SHIFTING FORMS FOR CLUMSY FELINES

OBSCURE ACADEMY #1

LAURA GREENWOOD

When she arrived at Obscure Academy, Krissi promised herself she'd focus on her studies and cheer practice. She wasn't going to worry about boys or the fact she's less than graceful in her leopard form.

Everything changes when she shares an accidental kiss with her flatmate, and despite every attempt to stay away from Jeremy, she keeps finding herself drawn back to the tiger shifter.

Can Jeremy convince her to give their relationship a chance?

-

Shifting Forms For Clumsy Felines is a light-hearted shifter academy m/f romance set at Obscure Academy. It is Krissi and Jeremy's complete story.

Krissi

THE WELCOME FAIR is buzzing with activity and various students calling for the freshers to join one society or another. I pay them no attention. I know exactly where I'm going and what I want to sign up for. All I need to do is find where they are. My ears prick as a whistle sounds and my whole body stands to attention as I wait for the cheer captain to call out what formation she wants us in. Until I realise I'm not a cheerleader at Obscure Academy.

At least, I'm not yet. Once I sign up and get through tryouts, that will change. And I've no doubt I'll manage. I may not be particularly graceful in my shifted form, but my human one can out-cartwheel anyone.

Even over the din of hundreds of students chatting and laughing, I can hear the cheers calling out to the part of me that lives to compete.

Now all I need to do is get to them so I can sign up.

"Hey." A tall guy with auburn hair waves at me. "It's Krystal, right?"

Eurgh, why does someone here already know my full name?

"I prefer Krissi," I correct him. "But yes. I'm sorry, I don't know your name." I can already feel my cheeks flaring with embarrassment.

"That's okay. I'm Jeremy. We live in the same flat."

"We do?" Oops. Maybe not the best thing to say. I always get like this around people I think are attractive, and there's no denying Jeremy is that.

And ripped. He's wearing a shirt, but I know athletes when I see them, and he definitely is one. Maybe I'll end up cheering for him at some point.

He smiles reassuringly at me. "We do. I saw your picture on the fridge."

"Ah." Which now seems like both a good idea, and a little bit of a creepy one. Only one of the others had put their photo up when I placed mine in the spot with my name. It's supposed to help us all recognise each other out and about, but I don't think it's working very well. "Are you a fresher too?"

He shakes his head. "I'm a second year."

"Doesn't it bother you that you've ended up sharing a flat with a group of freshers?" I barely want to share with first years, and I am one.

He shrugs. "Not really. Things don't get too serious until third year here."

"I'll take your word for it," I mumble.

"Have you signed up for anything yet?"

"I was looking for the cheer squad," I admit.

"I can take you over and introduce you to Zara if you want?" he offers.

For a moment, I think about saying no, but why should I? He seems nice, and we're going to be living together anyway. Besides, it's always good to be introduced to the captain by someone she knows.

"That sounds good. Are you sure you can leave?" I gesture to the stall he seems to be manning, only just realising it says *Obscure Academy Rugby Team* on the banner.

I guess I know what kind of athlete he is now. He certainly looks broad enough to be a rugby player.

"It's not a problem," he assures me. "Charlie, Steve, I'm just going to take Krissi over to see Zara."

One of the guys he calls to waves at him, acknowledging his words.

"They're going to let you just abandon your booth like that?" I ask.

He shrugs. "It's one of the advantages of being part of a team, there's always enough people."

"Unless you all come down with a mysterious illness," I retort. "It happened several times to our school's team."

Jeremy chuckles. "Let's guess, it always happened after a house party?"

"According to the rumours, it was after a lot of questionable behaviour. What always struck me as odd is that the humans and supernaturals all came down with the same thing at the same time."

"You don't have to worry about that here," he says.

"There might be a human among you. They're not banned from the academy."

"True. Though I'd like to think I'd notice. Humans smell different."

I raise an eyebrow, half wishing it wasn't considered rude to ask someone what kind of supernatural they are.

He guides me through the assembled students and towards a group of cheerleaders wearing a dark blue uniform with OA on the front of it. Even without talking to them, I know this is exactly what I'm looking for.

Jeremy waves at the redhead in front of everyone, and she saunters over, a sway in her hips that says she knows everyone is watching and she loves it.

"What's up, J?" she asks, not as flirtatiously as I expect given the way she's acting.

He clears his throat uncomfortably. "Hey, Zara. This is Krissi, one of my new flatmates. She wants to sign up for tryouts."

Zara's gaze rakes up and down me as she tries to make an assessment based on what she can see. I stand up straighter and hope it's enough for me to make a good impression. I don't want her to decide I'm not even worth giving a tryout to.

"Do you have any experience?" she asks.

I nod. "I've been training since I was seven, and was part of the team at King Edward's up until I came here."

She raises an eyebrow. "They're cup winners."

"Yes." I try to avoid sounding too prideful, but it's difficult. The team worked hard to win the championships several years in a row. I may not have been the captain of the team, but I still get to call myself a champion.

She clicks for one of the guys to come over with a clipboard and takes it from him. "Fill this out and we'll see you for tryouts at the end of the week."

Before I can ask her where I need to go for them,

she turns and walks off, leaving me alone with Jeremy and the clipboard.

"That went well," he says cheerily.

"It did?" I'm not sure what he was witness to, but I don't think anyone can say that went particularly well.

"She didn't scream at anyone, and you got what you wanted. For Zara, that's a good interaction."

"You're not filling me with confidence about working with her," I mutter.

"I suppose it depends how much you want to be a cheerleader."

I sigh. "It's been part of me for so long that I can't imagine *not* being one," I admit. "Is that weird?"

"Not at all."

"Some of the girls on my own squad said they thought it was. They used to say that being a leopard shifter should be more important than being a cheer-leader." The words are out before I can think about whether it's a good idea to say them to a stranger.

"You're a leopard?" he asks.

"I guess. But that doesn't really feel like me. If that makes any sense."

"It does," he assures me. "I'm a tiger shifter, but it's not how I'd describe myself first and foremost."

I raise an eyebrow. "It's not?" I think he's the first

fellow shifter I've met who feels the same way I do. Or he's the first to admit it out loud.

"No. I had a run-in with the former Shifter Queen that just cemented how I feel about it all. I don't *want* to be a shifter above everything else. I want to be me."

"You had a run-in with the Shifter Queen?" My mouth falls open and I stare at him, both amazed and confused at the same time.

"Not the current one," he says quickly. "I get on well with Kayra."

I stare at him, unable to formulate any of the questions racing around my head. "You know the current Shifter Queen too?"

"Yes. It was her mother that was the problem."

"Wasn't she deposed by Queen Kayra?"

"She was," he responds. "It's a long story. And not one for here." He glances around, reminding me that we're in the middle of the Freshers Fair. It's probably not the best place to be talking about the biggest political scandal to rock the shifter world since the 1800s.

"It sounds intriguing," I admit.

"Then I'll be glad to tell you it another time. But why don't we focus on the fair instead? You've signed up for cheer squad, what else do you want to be part of while you're here? There's ShiftSoc if you want to spend more time with shifters."

"What does a shifter social club even do? Shift and hang out in a room?"

"I think it's just an excuse to drink and party, like most of the societies." Laughter lingers in his voice. "But it's never a bad thing to be part of something like that."

"All right, then. Why don't you lead the way." I'm not sure whether I want to be part of it, but I promised my parents I'd make the most of my academy experience. Getting a social life is part of that, even if it's less important to me than my studies or cheer practice.

Despite my reservations, Obscure Academy is an experience I can only have once, and I don't want to miss anything while I'm here. Luckily for me, I seem to have found a guide who is determined to help me.

2

Krissi

"Take a break," Zara instructs, waving us all away.

I relax and let my arms fall to my sides. The fringe of my pom-poms tickles my thigh even through the workout leggings I'm wearing. I dread to think what they'll be like when I'm in uniform. It surprises me the academy isn't able to provide us with some that are better quality.

I head over to the benches to grab a drink. I'm not new to cheering. I know that if I want to stay on top form, then I need to stay hydrated.

"Hey," a girl I recognise from tryouts says as she grabs her water bottle.

"Hi." I wave at her, causing a rustle from my pom-pom.

"You're new too, right?"

I nod and drop my pom-poms on the bench so I can take a drink from my own. "I'm Krissi," I say, holding out my hand.

"Grace." She gives my hand a shake, then drops it quickly, probably because we're both sweaty from our workout. I'm not sure what I was thinking when I offered mine to her.

"What do you make of the Captain?" she asks.

I shrug. "She's tough, but she has to be."

"And how many cheer captains do you know who aren't?" Grace quips. "I've had my share of taskmasters."

"Same. I don't think you can get anywhere near competitive cheering without encountering a few."

"So true." She sighs. "I love it anyway."

"Me too. It's the perfect combination of gymnastics and…"

"Dance," she finishes for me. "I know what you mean. Mum pushed me towards ballet for the longest time, but it wasn't the right fit for me."

"Mine tried to get me to focus on gymnastics." I'd been terrible at it though. I know lots of people who are great at all the tumbling and tricks they need, but for me it wasn't quite right. When I got a chance to try out for my first cheer squad, everything fell into place.

"How are you finding the academy?" she asks.

"A little overwhelming," I admit. "What about you?" I take a long drink, enjoying the cold trickle of the water down my throat.

"Same. I'm looking forward to going out to Mixer with my flatmates on Friday night."

"Oh, we're going there too," I say. "Maybe I'll run into you."

"Probably when we've both had too much to drink and are in the middle of becoming best friends with a stranger in the toilets," Grace jokes.

A small snort escapes me. "It does seem to be a standard part of any night out."

She grins.

"Krissi!" someone calls before she's able to say anything else.

I turn to see Jeremy jogging towards me in his practice gear.

"Hey, I didn't realise you were practising now," I say.

"Every Monday evening so we're as ready as we can be for Wednesday's game. I see you're doing the same."

"Yes, though I think we're cheering for the

basketball team this week." I glance at Grace, but she just nods.

"Ah, that's a shame. I know I'll play better with you cheering from the sidelines." He grins, lighting up his face and giving him a boyish glow.

"I bet you say that to all the cheerleaders," I quip.

"Not so far," he counters. "But your squad is good, so I won't say it's a lie."

I let out a small laugh, surprisingly at ease with him. Maybe it's because I've seen him searching through the fridge for the milk first thing in the morning. I wouldn't have thought it was difficult to find, but he doesn't seem to be an early bird.

"Hopefully we're not going to disappoint," I mumble. "I'm not sure Zara is too impressed with us so far."

"Don't worry about Zara," he says quickly. "She just likes to put on a tough front."

Grace snorts. "That's one way of putting it."

"Jeremy!" One of the other rugby team members gestures at him from the other side of the field.

"I guess that's me," he says. "I'll catch you later?"

"Mmhmm. Have a good practice."

"You too." He gives me a small wave goodbye and hurries over to where the others are already warming up.

"So, who was that?" Grace asks when I turn back to her.

"Oh, he's Jeremy. He's a second year who lives in my flat."

"Does he have a girlfriend?" she asks, a knowing smile on her face.

"I don't think so, but it hasn't really come up."

Grace raises an eyebrow. "Really? Because I'd have thought with all the flirting going on that it would have been the first thing you'd have talked about."

"There wasn't any flirting," I deny quickly.

"Of course there wasn't." She all but winks at me.

I glance over my shoulder to where the rugby guys are hopping over small jumps one after the other. My gaze slips over them until I find Jeremy near the end. He's completely focused on his task and not even thinking about me anymore.

"We're flatmates," I assure her. "Nothing more."

"Yet," Grace teases.

"I'm not looking for anything serious." I want to focus on my classes and on cheering, I don't need the distraction a relationship will bring.

"Who said anything about serious? Just because you don't want to keep the car, it doesn't mean you can't take it for a test drive."

"I can't do that." My voice goes up an octave at the end.

"Why not? I don't think he's going to complain if you do," Grace responds. "And if you don't, then someone else is going to."

I flash one more look in Jeremy's direction and then shake my head.

"And you don't have to decide now," she points out. "You can keep harmlessly flirting for a while first. But be careful, or it'll lead to a drunken kiss and the next thing you know, you're waking up in his bed and discovering how badly he snores."

"Speaking from experience?" I ask.

Grace chuckles. "A bit."

"All right, break's over," Zara calls.

Grace sighs. "I guess it's time to make my muscles hate me tomorrow."

I let out a soft snort. "How about we make it up to them by going for a milkshake after practice?"

"I'll never say no to that."

The way she smiles at me makes me certain that I've found a friend.

My focus slips to the rugby pitch. Make that two friends.

And with the flat night out coming up at the end of the week, hopefully I'll make more.

3

Krissi

THE MOMENT I step inside my flat I breathe a sigh of relief and head towards the kitchen. I have plenty of work to do after my lectures today, but I want to start brewing my cup of tea before I head to my room.

"Hey, Krissi," Jeremy says as I step inside.

"Hey." I smile at him, pleased it's him in the kitchen. I don't dislike any of my flatmates, but he's the one I enjoy seeing the most. Maybe it's because we have a love of sports in common.

Or maybe it's something more.

I push the thought aside. I have enough to focus

on without adding a potential relationship into the mix.

"I just boiled the kettle, do you want a cup of tea?"

I nod. "Please. My mug's in..."

"The second cupboard. The purple mug with the polka dots, right?"

A warm fuzzy feeling fills me. "That's the one."

He pulls my mug out of the cupboard and goes through the motions of making me tea. After a couple of weeks living here, I know how to make everyone's tea and coffee, so it doesn't surprise me that he knows too.

"Good day?" he asks.

"Ish," I admit. "I'm struggling to understand some of the stuff my economics lecturer talks about, but I got some books out of the library, so I'm hoping that'll help." I dump my bag on the table and sit down so he knows I'm not about to run off and abandon him after he's so kindly made me tea.

"I could go through some of it with you?" Jeremy suggests. "It took me a while to understand it, so maybe I can help you."

"You did economics?"

He nods. "It was one of my modules last year. I was glad when it was open."

I chuckle. "I think I will be too. But I promised

Dad that I'd take at least one business module a term."

"Even if you're not interested in it?"

"It's a small price to pay for help with my tuition."

"Ah, right. I can understand that."

"Don't your parents have expectations of you?"

"My parents don't really pay much attention to me," he admits. "I'm the middle son. My older brother is already giving them grandchildren to occupy their time, and my younger brother is a musical prodigy. The most interesting thing about me is that I almost ended up engaged to the Shifter Queen."

"You say that like it's a bad thing." I hope he's going to tell me what happened there one day.

He lets out an uncomfortable laugh. "It is when she wasn't actually on board with the whole thing."

"I thought you said you were friends."

"We are. But that happened after. Kayra knows a thing or two about meddling parents."

A small pang of jealousy shoots through me at the way he says the other girl's name. I squash it down. I have no right to be jealous, and even if I did, he's already said they're just friends. I have no reason not to believe him.

"It must be hard to be the Queen."

Jeremy raises an eyebrow. "Most people talk about how good the parties and the clothes are."

I shrug. "It seems like there's a lot more to it than that to me. I'm sure the parties and clothes are nice, but that doesn't really mean anything when there's all the responsibility of being the monarch and all the people to look after."

"Maybe you could come with me next time I go to the palace?" he suggests, bringing two cups of steaming tea over and setting mine down in front of me before joining me at the table. "I think you and Kayra would get on well."

"I'm sure she has better things to do than meet me."

He chuckles. "I mostly go to social events," he promises.

"So I'll be going as your plus one?"

"Something like that."

I have to admit there's something appealing about the idea. "And everyone will be shifters there?" I wrap my hands around my mug and let the warmth sink into me.

"Probably. It's not unheard of for non-shifters to attend social events at the balls, but it's rare."

"I don't think they'll want someone with my poor shifting skills around."

"Are they really that bad?" he asks.

"Last time I shifted, I tried to walk along a very flat wall and I ended up falling off."

He chuckles. "I'm sorry, just the image of that is amusing."

I smile reassuringly at him, wanting him to know that there are no hard feelings for his reaction. "I saw the funny side after a while," I admit.

"We've all done something like that," he promises.

"I doubt it."

"It's true. Why else would there be a training agility course for shifters once a term?"

"There is?" That sounds intriguing. And useful for those like me who aren't necessarily the best when it comes to things that should come naturally to shifters.

Like being grateful and not falling off things.

"You don't already know?"

"Am I reacting like someone who does?" I take a sip of my tea.

"Ah, fair enough."

"This is good, by the way. Not everyone can make a good cup of tea."

"So true, have you tried Michaela's yet?"

I grimace at the mere memory of the witch's tea-making skills. "I don't think I've ever met someone who can manage to over brew tea and make it super weak at the same time. It's a special skill."

"She did tell me that her potion skills were bad at the beginning of term," Jeremy muses. "Perhaps that's why."

"That could be it."

"Anyway, the agility training," he prompts. "I can send you the information on it if you want?"

"Is it bad to say that I don't know if I do?"

Jeremy smiles, a warm look of understanding crossing over his face. Something about him constantly makes me feel at ease, as if I'm in a safe space where I won't be judged for anything I say or do. Even if that's admitting that I'm terrible at shifting despite being born with two forms.

"It's not bad at all," he assures me. "How about if you decide to go, I'll go with you? I'll even make sure to fall off a few things to make you look better."

A soft snort escapes me. "I don't think that's necessary, I'll be making a fool of myself enough for both of us."

"And in all likelihood, I'm not as good as I think I am anyway." He grins. "Isn't it strange that we're athletic in our human forms, but not as much in our shifted ones?"

"My theory was that the clumsiness all got directed into the wrong form and I was always supposed to be graceful as a shifter but something went wrong."

"That doesn't sound implausible."

"Though it could also just be that I've neglected my shifter side while focusing on my human talents and I've done it to myself."

"You sound like you think that's a bad thing?" He takes a drink while he waits for me to respond.

I take a moment to collect my thoughts. A small part of me is surprised I'm sharing them with him, but I've already got more in common with him than most people do, and I don't think there's anything wrong with the two of us exploring that connection so long as it doesn't distract me from my studies and cheerleading practice.

"I'm not sure whether it's a bad thing or not," I admit. "Sometimes I feel like it is. And like I've brought this on myself." A stray strand of dark brown hair falls in front of my eyes. I reach up and push it back, which seems to draw Jeremy's attention to my face.

"Maybe it doesn't matter if it's your fault or not," he suggests. "If you're happy with the person you are, then who cares whether it was you who did it to yourself, or if it's just something nature decided. All you have to do is make the most of the talents you've been given. And I've seen you cheering, you have talent."

"You've been watching me cheer?"

He grimaces. "Sorry, that sounds a bit creepy, doesn't it? I promise it isn't. I just catch sight of the squad when there's a break in our practice."

"It's okay, I understand," I promise. "I watch your rugby practice during breaks sometimes."

He raises an eyebrow, seemingly surprised that I've admitted to something like that. To be honest, I am too. Jeremy doesn't seem like the kind of guy who would take advantage of a situation, but I'm not used to being this freely spoken around anyone. I had friends at my old school, but they never really liked it when I delved deeper into my shifter problems. Probably because they didn't see them as real problems.

But now I'm sitting across from someone who understands. More than that, someone who comprehends what I'm talking about and sees past it.

"I'll think about the agility training," I promise. "And if I do go, then I'm holding you to your promise and you're coming with me."

Jeremy chuckles and drains the rest of his tea. "You have my word. And let me know if you want help with the economics stuff."

I let out a small groan. "I almost managed to forget about that."

"You can put it off for tonight?" he suggests. "Get yourself a pizza and watch a film or something like that? Just because you're here to learn doesn't mean you have to do it all the time."

"Spoken like a true second year," I tease.

"I owe it to you all to pass on my wisdom," he retorts. "Or else I wasted all that time for nothing."

I shake my head in bemusement, glad I've found someone who is so easy to spend time with. Though if I'm not careful, I'm going to find myself falling for him without realising it. I've seen enough movies to know how these things go.

Jeremy gets to his feet and picks up his mug. "Are you done with yours? I'll wash it at the same time."

I nod and hand it to him. Our fingers brush against one another as he takes it from me, causing butterflies to erupt into life in my stomach.

Perhaps it's too late to avoid potential feelings, but I'll cross that bridge when I get to it and not a moment sooner.

4

Krissi

THE KITCHEN IS the loudest I've ever heard it, and far more full than it has any right to be. To say the flat is built for nine people, it shouldn't only take six to fill up the kitchen. "Who are we missing?" Essie asks, slurring her words more than she should be. It takes a lot to get a supernatural drunk, and she's well on her way to it.

I can't say I'm too far behind.

"Bernie said she was joining us after class," Michaela says.

"Oh yeah, it must suck to be a vampire," Essie responds. "They have to cram all of their lessons into a shorter space of time, and then if they want to hang out with anyone who isn't a vampire, they have to move straight on to that."

"Being able to heal easily and not ageing at the same rate sound good to me," Michaela mutters.

"Me too," I agree.

The other girls turn to look at me with surprise written all over their faces. "Don't you have good healing? You're a shifter."

"It's never felt that way when I've hurt myself," I admit.

"But Bernie only makes seven of us, who else is missing?" Essie says as she looks around the room and tries to work it out.

"Jeremy," I say, realising that the other shifter is missing. "He must be at practice still."

"And the guy from room eight?" Fiona suggests, surprising me. The mermaid seems to be the most reserved of all of us, though maybe it's just because it's early in the term and we're just starting to get to know one another.

A collective noise of assent goes around us.

"I don't think I've ever talked to him," Michaela admits. "Have you?"

I shake my head. "I think he's called Craig, though?"

"Maybe he's a ghost?" Essie suggests. "They're real."

"Only one way to find out," Michaela responds. "Hey, Dylan."

The reaper pulls his attention away from the game the boys are playing and slides down the bench. "You said my name?"

"We wanted to ask you about Craig," Michaela says.

He frowns. "I'm not sure I can help, I don't know anything about him."

"Oh." Michaela slumps back in her seat. "I was hoping he was a ghost or something."

Dylan chuckles. "I'm afraid not. There aren't enough humans around here for there to be any ghosts. There are loads in the town centre though."

"That must be so cool to be able to see them," she says.

He grimaces. "Not really."

"So you don't know anything about Craig?" I prompt, hoping it takes him away from the subject he's clearly uncomfortable with.

"Nothing. What about you?" he asks Cyprus, inviting the other guy into the conversation.

"Nope, he's a mystery," Cyprus says. "I thought I saw him go into his room once. And Jeremy says that he can hear him on the other side of the wall."

"Oh and there was food in the fridge," Fiona pipes up. "Some leftover chicken or something like that."

"You mean today?" Dylan asks, a horrified expression on his face.

"Yes, why?"

"I kind of threw it away."

The whole table goes silent as his words sink in.

"Oops?" Michaela offers.

"It looked like it was turning bad," he responds. "I didn't realise it was Craig's."

"We can replace it on our way back tonight," I say. "It was from the chicken place across the road, right?"

He nods.

"Great, then we'll just get some more tonight, problem solved."

He smiles at me, seeming more reassured than before.

The door opens and I turn my attention towards it, hoping that it's Jeremy walking in.

"Oh phew, you're still here," Bernie says.

"We're barely getting started," Michaela assures the vampire. "Grab a seat and grab a drink, we're going to get you druunnnnk."

Bernie chuckles. "All right, just let me go get changed and I'll join you." She disappears again, though I know she'll be back quickly, she doesn't take very long to get ready.

"All right, let's get this party started properly," Michaela says. "What do you think, Ring Of Fire?"

We all groan. It may only have been a couple of weeks since term started, but we've already learned how deadly this game can be.

And how fun it can be.

"I'll grab the cards," Cyprus says, getting to his feet and grabbing them.

Michaela places a pint glass in the middle of the table and we all help spread the cards around it with their faces down.

The door opens but I don't look up this time, expecting that it's Bernie returning right up until there's a whiff of cologne right by me.

"Hey," Jeremy says softly.

I turn to face him, a small smile on my face. "Hey," I return. "You look good." The words are out before I think twice about it. His open-necked shirt fits him well, which isn't a surprise given the rugby induced muscles he's sporting.

"And you look gorgeous," he responds.

A blush creeps to my cheeks and I pull down the admittedly short skirt of my dress. I know I look good, but there's something different about Jeremy saying it than someone else. "Thank you."

"Whoo, Bernie!" Michaela calls as the vampire reenters the room. "We're all here, that means it's time to start."

Bernie chuckles. "It doesn't seem like you've been waiting for me too hard." She pours herself a healthy measure of vodka into a glass and tops it up with tomato juice.

I wrinkle my nose. I hope I'm not going to have to drink a dirty pint with that in later, I can't stand tomato juice.

"Will you hand me the tabasco?" she asks Cyprus.

He nods and tosses it over to her to add to her drink. That's going to be vile when added in with everything else.

"All right, I'll start," Michaela calls. "We have a couple of hours until the taxis come to take us to the club, so that gives us plenty of time."

"Did someone at least invite Craig tonight?" Dylan asks.

"We put a note on the fridge." I wave towards it.

"Seven," Michaela calls, holding up the seven of clubs. "Boo, that's a boring one."

"Yes, but you get to control it," Bernie points out.

"What's seven again?" Jeremy whispers to me.

"Heaven. When Michaela points to the ceiling, we all have to, and the last person has to drink," I say.

"Has to *what?*" Essie asks with a teasing note in her voice.

I groan. "I'm no good at drinking games."

"That's twice! You need to take two consumptions of your beverage," she responds.

"You sound ridiculous," I point out, being careful to pick up my glass with my left hand so I don't get dinged again.

"I have an eight," Fiona says, holding up her card. "And I pick Dylan."

"What did I ever do to you?" the reaper asks.

"Nothing, you just seem the most sober."

He chuckles and leans back in his seat, not protesting too much about the fact he has to drink every time she does. The game may be competitive, but it's also a lot of fun.

My voice grows hoarse from the shouting and laughter that ensue. By the time we get to the club, I'm going to be ready to dance the night away without a care in the world.

And I can't wait.

5

Jeremy

It's hard to make sense of anything happening in the club with the music pounding and the swaying bodies of hundreds of students. Not all of them are from Obscure Academy, but I recognise a lot of them from my lectures or from around.

Someone bumps into me and I turn to apologise before realising it's Krissi. Her cheeks are flushed with a combination of the heat and the drinks she's been putting back, but it only makes her more beautiful.

Though apparently clumsier too.

"Do you want to get some air?" she yells over the music.

If I didn't have decent hearing thanks to my inner tiger shifter, I don't think I'd have heard her.

I nod and hold out my hand to her. If I was sober, I'd know better than to touch her like that. But as far as Krissi's concerned, I find it hard to ignore the draw I feel to her.

She slips her hand into mine and I try to control my reaction to such a simple gesture. I always knew that Kayra choosing Magnus over me was the right thing for her, but meeting Krissi has finally made it clear that it was the right thing for me too.

Not that I envy Magnus his position while Kayra is still trying to cement herself properly as the Shifter Queen, especially after she went and changed some of the rules about how the community runs. Most of that isn't felt by people at our level, but I know they're happening.

I lead Krissi through the club and out into the smoking area. I hate that this is the best place to get air here, but it's better than nothing.

"Sorry, I think the heat was getting to me," Krissi says, fanning her face.

"I know what you mean." My ears are ringing in the relative quiet compared to the music pounding away inside.

Krissi groans and presses her hands against her ears. "I wish they considered how bad it is for shifters to have music that loud."

"They do at Jungle."

"You mean that shifter only place?"

"That's the one. I've never been, but one of the guys on the team told me about it," I say.

"Just with shifters?"

"Allegedly, they even have a room where you can shift and dance at the same time." Up until now, it's never sounded fun, but seeing the expression on her face, I think it might be.

"We should go some time. I'd like to see that. Not that I can dance very well as a leopard. I might as well just lie down and bob my head."

"Are you saying that what you were doing in there as a human was good dancing?" I tease.

She makes a little shocked face. "Jeremy, you wound me." She presses her hands to her chest, only serving to draw my attention to how tight her dress is and how well it fits her. Between the hours of weekly cheer practice, and the shifter genetics, she's at peak fitness, and while she's dressed like this, it's obvious.

I'm glad I'm not the jealous type or I might struggle with it, even if she is just my friend.

"Sorry, what I meant to say is that you're the best

dancer I've ever seen."

Krissi lets out a soft snort. "Now I know you're lying to me."

"I'd never lie to you."

Her entire demeanour softens and she reaches out to put a hand on my chest. "I know you wouldn't."

Pride wells up within me at the idea that I've managed to prove to her that I'm trustworthy. I want her to think well of me, and not just because I want to kiss her right now.

She's standing close enough, and she's leaning in. Everything about her body language says that she wants this.

And while that may be true, I'm not going to take advantage of the situation. If we have a first kiss, and I hope we do, then it's going to be when both of us are sober and able to make our choice with open eyes.

As hard as it is to do, I take a step back and clear my throat. "I think I'm about ready to go home."

She nods. "Me too. Mickie has already banned me from going near the bar again."

"I'm not sure why, she's easily as drunk as the rest of us."

Krissi grins. "And I can deal with drinking better

than any witch can." She sways as she talks, revealing that it may be a lie.

Then again, I haven't seen Michaela in about half an hour, there's a chance Krissi is right and she's in a worse state than the shifter in front of me.

It's been a fun night, but I think it's time that we all went home.

I pull out my phone and open up the group chat and type out a quick message asking who else is ready. If it's just the two of us, then we can just grab a taxi or something.

Krissi's phone pings and she opens up her bag to pull it out despite having just seen me send the message.

She laughs lightly as she realises what she's done. "Oops. But look, Mickie's already replied. She says she and Fiona already. Oh and Dylan sent an eggplant emoji. I'm not sure what that means."

I try to smother a laugh, but she catches me.

Krissi cocks her head to the side. "Do you know what it means?"

"Yes."

"So...oh. OH." She blushes furiously. "Right, sorry, I knew that."

"At least he's not saying anything obscene."

"Somehow this is worse," she mutters. "Couldn't he just have said he's gone home?"

"Have you met Dylan? He's never going to take that route," I point out. I like the guy, but he does have an annoying tendency of overusing emojis, particularly when he's been drinking. I wonder if it's so no one can tell he's unable to type anymore.

"Fair point." She sighs. "Let's go, we can meet the others outside the club." She turns without waiting for me to respond and starts to make her way back inside.

I hurry after her, a little worried that she's going to fall over on her way out. She may be graceful and sturdy when she's sober, but it turns out that drunk-Krissi is neither of those things.

It makes me wonder just how bad things really are when she's in her shifter form.

6

Krissi

I HOLD out my arms in an attempt to balance myself as I walk down the curb, refusing to use the path because of reasons that are lost to me.

"You're going to hurt yourself," Michaela calls through cackles of laughter.

"No, I'm not!"

"We need to get some food in her," she mutters to Cyprus and Jeremy.

"Are you sure she won't just throw it all up?" Fiona asks.

"Ew, I'm not cleaning it up if she does," Cyprus responds.

I spin around, easily keeping my balance.

Ish.

"I'm not going to throw up," I assure him. "I'm perfectly fine. I'll just do this and my head will be clear." I reach within myself and pull my leopard to the surface.

My whole body changes, with fur sprouting all over my skin, and everything getting bigger until I'm standing in front of them in my feline form.

Or I am, until I start to fall over.

A blur of orange and black streaks towards me from where Jeremy stands, propping me up before I fall over completely.

"Shift back, Krissi," Michaela says. "You're just going to hurt yourself."

"And it's illegal to be shifted on the street," Cyprus adds.

His words are all it takes to cut through the drunken haze and I force myself back into my human form.

"Whoa, a little warning would be nice," Cyprus mutters. "I don't want to accidentally see you naked or anything."

"That's not going to happen." I pull at the fabric of my dress. "Magic clothes. They're great. Especially when you don't want to end up naked in front of guys you...people."

Michaela raises an eyebrow and shoots a look past me to where Jeremy has also returned to human form.

"You really are clumsy as a leopard, aren't you?" he asks.

I chuckle nervously, feeling a little less drunk after my shift. My logic is sound, it's my actions that are a bit more questionable. "Would you believe me if I said it was the booze?"

"Do you want me to?"

"All right, you two, quit the flirting and let's not linger in case anyone saw you being all big catty," Michaela says, reaching out and hooking her arm through mine.

"We're not flirting," I protest loudly. "We're not."

"Muuhmm. And if you keep telling yourself while actually flirting like it's going out of fashion, then you're going to end up in bed with him by the end of the month."

A blush rises to my cheeks. "Will not."

Michaela sighs and draws me further away from the others who seem to have started a conversation about how awesome Jeremy looks shifted. I wish I hadn't been too busy falling over to see it.

"Do you really want me to go all truth bomb on you?" she asks.

"That depends, are you making it? Cause I've

heard you're bad at that stuff." Oops, maybe I'm still drunker than I think I am.

To my surprise, Michaela laughs. "It's not a potion."

"In which case, bring it on."

"If you like him, you should stop messing around and do something about it. I'm not saying you have to marry the guy or anything, just go on a date with him or something. It's mean to lead him on."

My mouth falls open and I struggle to find the words I need. "I'm not leading him on," I murmur eventually.

"Maybe not on purpose, but anyone with eyes can see the two of you are into each other. The only person who doesn't seem to know is you."

"And Jeremy..."

"Oh no, he definitely knows." She tries to wink at me, but does a terrible job of it. "Drunk Michaela is here for the next few hours to drop all the truth bombs you needs," she promises.

"So if I want you to ever talk sense into me, all I need to do is buy you a few drinks?" I ask.

"Talking sense is something I'll do for free," she promises.

I shake my head in bemusement.

"Look, I like you, I like Jeremy, I don't want to see

either of you get hurt, but you're heading that way if you're not careful."

"I'm not looking for anything serious."

"Famous last words," she sing-songs. "But you know it's not bad to be in a relationship."

"But it is if I want to focus on classes and cheering and..."

"Krissi," she says firmly, cutting off my rambling. "Aren't you here to have fun?"

"Well, yes."

"Then have fun."

"Chicken!" Cyprus yells, pushing through us and heading towards the fast food place next to campus.

"Don't forget to get replacement chicken for Craig," I call out.

Michaela chuckles. "Think about it. I'll make sure Cyprus buys extra chicken." She heads inside after him without waiting for me to respond.

"Are you okay?" Jeremy asks as he comes to stand beside me, leaving the others to get their chicken.

I nod. "Thanks for propping me up, I could have really hurt myself back there."

"You're welcome. I'm glad I could help."

"But you shouldn't have shifted. If we'd have gotten caught..."

"Nothing bad would have happened," he assures

me. "Unless you have a past of public shifting you haven't told me about."

"I don't. I'm not sure what came over me."

"A little bit too much to drink," he says. "How's your head now?"

"A lot clearer. Yours?"

"Same. The unplanned shift really helped with that. I'll be thanking you in the morning." He grins. "Do you not want chicken?"

I shake my head. "I always regret it in the morning. I prefer to eat my hangover cures for breakfast."

"Please tell me it isn't raw egg?"

I laugh lightly. "No. I make steak and eggs."

"That sounds good."

"If you're in the flat at ten tomorrow, I can make you some," I offer without thinking twice about it. Maybe I should after what Michaela said.

"I can be there."

The way he smiles at me makes me feel warm and fuzzy inside, though perhaps that's just the alcohol still buzzing around my system. I'm not naive enough to think that I've miraculously become sober in the past fifteen minutes, even with a shift.

The others pile out of the chicken shop with their boxes of greasy goodness in their hands and wide smiles on their faces. We start making our way back onto campus, chattering about the events of the night as we go.

"Where did Dylan get to?" I ask.

"He went home with one of the girls from his chemistry class," Fiona answers. "And Essie went home too drunk. Who knew a fae who couldn't hold their drink."

"I don't think any of us can claim that after tonight," I mutter.

She laughs lightly. "You may have a point."

Cyprus slots his key into the door and holds it open for us so we can all head through.

"I'll see you in the morning," I call to my flatmates heading into the kitchen to eat their chicken. They're probably going to be awake for hours, and now my shift has helped sober me up, I'm tired.

"Night, Krissi," Michaela calls.

"I'm heading to bed too," Jeremy says, no doubt experiencing something similar to me. "See you later."

They wave and disappear, probably wanting to avoid their food getting cold.

"I'll see you for breakfast," Jeremy says.

"It's a date." I wince as soon as the words are out of my mouth, realising this is exactly what Michaela means about giving off mixed signals.

There's no taking them back. Whatever happens, I'm looking forward to breakfast with him.

Once I've completely sobered up, I'm going to have to do some serious thinking about what I want. But for now, I need to sleep.

7

Krissi

My alarm blares out, waking me from a surprisingly deep slumber. I open my eyes slowly, fully expecting there to be a headache and the other signs of the alcohol consumption of the night before.

Luckily for me, I seem to have escaped hangover-free, probably because of the ill-advised shift on the way home.

I let out a soft groan. What made me think that was a good idea?

I throw the covers off and quickly shower and dress. Normally, I'd probably go to the kitchen without doing that, but I'm conscious that I'll be having breakfast with Jeremy.

Maybe that should be an indication of something, but I don't have the time to dwell on it right now.

No one else is around when I get to the kitchen, probably because they're either at their lectures already, or they're in their rooms nursing their heads.

I lay out all of my ingredients and fill the kettle with water while humming to myself.

The door creaks and I glance over my shoulder to see Jeremy walking in, looking surprisingly clear-headed.

Which makes sense now I think about it, he shifted too.

"Morning," he says cheerfully.

"Morning," I respond.

"Want me to make tea while you cook?"

Ah, so he's noticed that I've already started prepping. "Sounds good."

He grabs our mugs and starts to make the drinks while I turn my attention to the meat.

"How's your hangover?" he asks.

"Pretty much non-existent," I admit.

"Probably a result of the shift."

"I still can't believe I did that. I've never been

the kind of shifter who did things like that," I lament.

Jeremy chuckles. "Alcohol does funny things to people."

"Even so. It's driven into us our entire lives that we're supposed to keep these things off the streets." I crack a couple of eggs and drop them into a mug so I can whisk them up before remembering two of us are eating and adding a couple more.

"There are loads of shifters who flout those laws."

"Yeah, the foxes or birds. They're not going to get caught running around. Someone's going to notice if a leopard starts walking down the street in the middle of Yorkshire."

He gives an amused laugh. "That's fair. But humans know about us."

"That doesn't change the law," I point out.

"True. But it does make it a bit restrictive."

"At least it isn't a couple of hundred years ago when I could have been tried for treason for breaking the secrecy laws," I mutter as I pull out the pan and set it on the burner.

"Exactly, look on the bright side."

I sigh. "Did I do anything else dumb last night?"

"Not that I'm aware of. We all just danced and had a good time."

"Hmm."

"Except for Dylan. He disappeared off with the girl he's sort-of-seeing."

"So he had the best time of us all," I quip. I pour the whisked eggs into the pan and start the process of scrambling them. I turn on the grill and slide in the steak.

"He might not, he makes it sound as if she has crazy eyes," Jeremy says.

"There's no such thing as crazy eyes."

He finishes making our tea and takes it over to the table. "Do you want anything else? I think I have some orange juice left."

"Oh, that'd be nice if you do." Somehow this is turning from a casual hangover breakfast between flatmates to something more.

I'm honestly not sure what to make of it, but I can't fully shake Michaela's words from last night. I know that we can't keep doing this.

I dish up our food and follow him over to the table, setting it down just as he finishes pouring us a couple of glasses of orange juice. I flash him a grateful smile and we sit down.

"What lecture do you have?" I ask.

"Supernaturals in the middle ages."

"I don't know if that sounds dreadfully boring, or fascinating."

He laughs lightly. "You'd be right on both. The

lectures can be a bit dull, but when Professor Sherbs takes the seminars, you can see how much he cares about the subject, and then it's interesting."

"But not when he lectures on it?" I take a bite of steak and eggs, enjoying the savoury taste that'll get rid of any lingering effects of last night's overindulgences. It does a much better job than fried chicken for me, I'm not sure why.

"I assume his students do well in their exams because of the seminars, so no one ever questions it."

"Ah, that makes sense. So is that what you want to do when you leave here? History?"

He nods. "I think so. I've always wanted to work with old documents trying to find what secrets they have in them."

"That sounds like a super-specific career choice."

"It is, but that's why I came here and not Sabre Woods Academy."

I raise an eyebrow. Most people come to Obscure Academy because they can't get into their first choice.

"The supernatural history department here is the best in the country. And it focuses on all of us instead of just big cats, which is what I want to do," he explains without me even needing to ask.

"I didn't know that."

"Not many people do. What do you want to do after you leave?"

"I'm not sure yet," I admit. "I know that's bad, but I hoped I'd find something that connected with me during my classes."

"Have you?" He takes a bite of his food.

"Not yet."

"There's still time."

"I know. I'm trying not to worry about it." I polish off the rest of my food and reach for my orange juice to wash it down.

"You shouldn't. It's just your first year, you don't have to worry about any of this yet."

Ah, somehow I forgot he's a second year. I think it stops meaning anything after a while.

"This is delicious, by the way." He gestures to his plate.

"Thanks." A small blush rises to my cheeks. "It's nothing fancy."

"Sometimes, food doesn't have to be. Simple can be tasty."

"I'm glad you think that, because I'm not a very inventive cook. I can do a few things well, but you won't get any variety for me." It isn't until the words are out of my mouth that I realise I'm making an assumption about whether we'll eat together again.

"Then let's just hope they're different dishes to the ones I'm capable of making."

I let out a light laugh. "There's always takeaway."

"We're students," he reminds me. "We have to cook or we'll run out of money."

"Ah. Yeah, that's a problem. Though can we really complain when we've just eaten steak?"

"We're big cats. We have to eat it."

"You know that's not true." Amusement dances through my voice. "We could eat vegetarian if we wanted."

He wrinkles his nose. "I'd miss meat too much."

"Me too. But that doesn't mean we wouldn't be capable of it. Our digestive systems in these forms work the same as humans. It'd be more of a problem if we were living mostly as our big cat selves."

"True," he agrees.

Before we can continue our conversation, the door to the kitchen swings open and Michaela pops her head around. "Oh good, you're still here," she says.

"What's up?" I ask.

"I was about to leave for our lecture, are you ready to go?"

I glance at the clock on the wall and my eyes widen. "I hadn't realised the time. I'm coming. I'll do the dishes when I get back."

"I'll do them," Jeremy promises. "You cooked, it's only fair that I clean up. And my lecture isn't for another hour."

"Thanks." I beam at him, glad to feel like I'm part of a team. "I'll see you in a bit."

"See you." He starts collecting up the plates.

"I just need to grab my bag, but then I'm ready," I promise Michaela.

"Okay, but do it quietly, my head is killing me."

"Don't you have a potion or something you can take for it?"

"Not that I can brew myself," she mutters. "But I might be able to get one off a friend."

"Before the lecture?" I pop in to my room and grab my bag, not letting the door close while I do.

"Sadly not. What about you? Any after effects, or did your shift do exactly what you said it did?" She waits as I lock my door and then starts heading down the corridor towards the exit of our flat. Judging from the state of her hair, I suspect she hasn't been awake long.

"It worked," I say. "I'll have to remember it and shift when I get back to my room next time I go on a night out."

"Not on the street again?" she jokes.

"I'm going to try not to, but I wasn't thinking completely rationally at the time."

"Somehow, I'm not surprised."

We move on to dissecting the rest of the night, though it really does seem as if Jeremy is right about what happened. We all went out, had some drinks, and danced. But that's what makes it fun. I want to be able to spend time with my flatmates like this.

I just hope that next time I do better at not making a complete fool of myself in the process.

8

Krissi

"WANT TO GRAB A COFFEE BEFORE PRACTICE?" I ask Grace.

"For all that flies, yes," she half-groans. "I'm still hungover from last night."

"Did you have a good time? I didn't see you." Even though I had a great time with my flatmates last night, I did hope to run into my friend too.

"It was fun," she says. "But I think I have more fun at cheer events."

"That makes sense. We have more in common." We head into the coffee shop and a cheery woman waves us over.

"I hope she has a hangover cure coffee," Grace mutters.

"That bad? It's been hours."

"I'm surprised you're not feeling worse. Did you not drink much?"

"I drank plenty," I admit with a grimace. "But I may have made an ill-advised shift on the streets and it cleared my mind."

"Lucky," she mutters. "I wish I could do that."

I raise an eyebrow, wondering if this is when she's going to tell me what she is. It's rude to ask, so it's always better to wait until someone volunteers the information.

"Welcome to Pixie Cups," the woman says. "What can I get for you?"

"Is there anything that's good for hangovers?" Grace asks.

The woman's lips quirk into an amused smile. "It's one of my most popular requests. You can add a shot to any of our coffees for just fifty pence."

"Great, then I'll take a skinny latte with a shot of that, please," Grace says before turning to me. "What about you?"

"Chai tea, please."

"Do you want an extra shot in that?" the barista asks, gesturing to the board behind her.

I scan down the options, noting the wide variety,

including a shot of alertness, and a shot of clarity. I'm not sure how those things are different, but I'm impressed by the array on offer, I don't think our magical coffee shop at home does this many.

"I'm okay, thanks."

"No problem." She turns from us and starts making our drinks.

"Your shift must have really helped your head," Grace says.

"I also had breakfast with Jeremy."

She raises an eyebrow. "Rugby player, Jeremy?"

"You know which Jeremy," I point out. "You've met him multiple times."

"Mmhmm, but you keep insisting there's nothing going on between the two of you."

"And breakfast doesn't count as anything. We were both drinking last night and he helped me during the unfortunate shifting incident. I thought I'd help him with the remains of his hangover."

"And there's nothing else?" she prompts.

I sigh. "Mickie said that she thought there was something between us and that I shouldn't be leading him on."

Curiosity darts across Grace's face. "Do you think you are?"

"Not intentionally. I mean, I do think I like him as more than just a friend." I can hardly believe the words are leaving my mouth, but I know they're true, and it feels good to be talking about him. "But I promised myself that I'd focus on other things and not jump into a relationship when I came here."

"Sometimes these things just can't be predicted," Grace points out. "You have to go with the flow.

"Maybe."

The barista returns with two takeaway cups in her hand and sets them down in front of us. "Here you go," she says. "How do you want to pay?"

"One second, I think I have cash," I say, reaching for my bag.

Grace shakes her head. "I've got these ones. You can buy next time." She brings up the payment app on her phone and scans it over the payment machine. It beeps loudly.

"Thank you," the barista responds with a more genuine smile than ever. She's probably pleased that we're already talking about coming back. "You can download our app if you want loyalty points too, there's a code on each of your cups."

"Thanks," I say. It sounds like a good idea, especially if we're going to end up coming here a lot.

We grab our drinks and make our way outside, heading in the direction of the practice field.

Grace takes a sip of her coffee. "Ow. Hot. But so good, I can feel the hangover fading already."

"I don't think it works that quickly," I point out. "It's probably just the placebo effect."

"Spoilsport. It's magic, you don't know how quickly it works."

She has a point. Despite being around other supernaturals, as well as humans, my entire life, I'm only really aware of how shifters work when it comes to magic. I suppose to some extent, I've never had to worry about it much.

"Oh, look who it is," Grace says, calling my attention to the street.

I look up to find the person I want to see the most, and want to see the least, standing in front of me by the road crossing.

"Hey, Krissi."

"Jeremy, hey," I say, smiling at him, and hoping it covers up the nerves I'm feeling considering the topic of my conversation with Grace.

My friend flashes me a knowing smile, as if she's pleased this is happening.

"We're just heading to cheer practice," I tell him needlessly. He knows what my gym bag looks like by this point.

"I'm on my way to the library, I have an exam coming up and I'm nowhere near ready for it."

"Maybe you should pick up a coffee with a shot

of alertness from Pixie Cups," I suggest, gesturing with my cup.

"Good idea." Something about the way he's talking makes me think he's just as nervous as I am. "Oh, I meant to ask you this morning, but are you still interested in that shifter agility training? The details just got released and I wondered if you wanted to go."

"When is it?" I ask.

"I'll have to check, but it's not far away." He shrugs. "It'll come around again if you're busy this time."

"She'll go," Grace pipes up. "She needs the training."

Jeremy chuckles. "She did almost fall over in leopard form last night."

I bite my lip nervously. "If you hadn't shifted and helped me stay upright, I think I'd have been flat on my back." I tuck a stray strand of hair behind my ear.

"Always here to help," he says cheerily.

I give a small laugh and smile at him. "Sign us up, it'll be fun."

"I certainly hope so." He looks at me for a moment longer than is necessary. "Anyway, I'll see you back at the flat?"

I nod.

"Have a good cheer practice."

"Enjoy studying," I respond before wincing. How many people actually *like* preparing for a test?

"I'll try. A coffee will definitely help with that." He waves goodbye and heads off towards the coffee shop.

I glance over my shoulder to watch him go.

"So, want to tell me what's really going on?" Grace asks. "Did you wake up in the same bed this morning or something?"

"What? No. Nothing like that." We start walking again, hastening our paces so we don't end up late for practice.

"So..."

I sigh. "It's complicated."

"It's really not. You like him, he likes you, it couldn't be more simple."

"I don't know that he likes me," I mutter.

"Then you can't be looking very hard for the information," she says. "Because it's painfully obvious how much you two like each other from the way you interact with one another."

"I didn't know that."

"Obviously," she says sternly. "I think you should listen to me, and to your flatmate. You're going to have to make an actual decision about this or you're going to end up regretting it for the rest of your life. Jeremy will become the one that got away."

I frown. There's a lot of truth in her words, but that doesn't mean I'm completely on board yet.

"I'll think about it."

"Good. But don't take too long, and tell me when you make a decision."

"Do you really think I won't?"

Grace smiles and links her arm through mine. "Nope. You're my best friend, and I'm yours. There's no getting away with not telling me anything."

A sense of security rolls over me at her words and I realise that's how I've been thinking about Grace for a few weeks now. It's amazing how quickly bonds have formed since coming to Obscure Academy.

I'm lucky to have met so many good people, even if I have ended up in a confusing situation when it comes to my love life as a result.

9

Krissi

I TRY NOT to get too frustrated over the swimming words on the page in front of me. I've been trying to get the rules of the Shifter Paradox through my head for hours, and I'm not getting anywhere.

My phone buzzes and I turn it over to find a message in the group chat with Jeremy's picture next to it.

< Anyone want anything from the kitchen? >

I type back without thinking about it. < Tea would be nice, if you don't mind? >

< Coming right up! >

I smile and put my phone back down, turning my

attention back to the textbook in front of me. I'm going to get to the bottom of this if it's the last thing I do.

Five minutes later, there's a knock on my door.

"Come in," I call.

Jeremy pushes it open with his back, two steaming mugs in his hand. He sets one down on the desk.

"You all right? You look like you're about to scream at your book." Concern lingers in his voice.

"I am," I mutter. "We've been learning about the Shifter Paradox and I just can't get my head around it."

"Oh yeah, I struggled with that one too. I think it's because we're shifters. It seems so contrary to what we've grown up knowing."

"That doesn't help me understand it," I point out.

He chuckles. "That's fair. Do you want me to go through it with you?"

"Do you have time?" Hope blossoms within me, and I don't think it's because I might finally understand what the paradox is supposed to be about either.

"I'm not doing anything important."

I sigh. "Tea and private tutoring, how are you single?" The moment the words are out of my mouth before I can think twice about them. "I'm sorry, I didn't mean that."

"It's fine," he mumbles. "So what's the problem?" He sets his tea down at my desk and looks over my shoulder at the textbook.

"I just don't get it. What's the paradox even supposed to be about and why does it matter?"

"The why it matters is the easy part," he responds. "We have to learn this because it's the way the world works and if we understand that, then a lot of things fall into place."

"Hmm."

"You don't agree?"

"I think the world can be a miserable place whether we want it to be or not."

"I thought you were supposed to be a *cheer*leader."

I groan and throw him a disapproving look. "You know that's not why we're called that."

"I do, but I wanted to see your face when I said it." He grins at me as if it really is as simple as that.

"Okay, so that's why I'm supposed to know about the paradox, but it doesn't explain what it is."

"I suspect you already know. The paradox is simply that we change size, but that doesn't make much sense. How can something as small as a mouse or as big as an elephant be hiding within a human body?"

"That's like asking where a harpy stores their wings."

"In their backs, I imagine. But that's a whole other factor to take into account. Harpies are connected to their wings in a way we're not to our forms. We fully shift when we change into our animals. They don't."

I frown. What he's saying makes sense, even if I think it's a little strange to look at things that way.

"Do you have some paper?" he asks.

"Sure." I scoot around on my desk chair and lean over, not realising quite how close it would bring the two of us.

We're barely inches apart, and neither of us moves. There's something in his eyes that invites me in and makes me feel as if he sees me in a way not many people have before.

I'm not sure which of us makes the first move, but suddenly his hand is cupping my cheek and his lips are pressed against mine.

I lose myself in the moment, my whole body tingling with the excitement of a first kiss. I've thought about what kissing Jeremy would be like more times than I want to admit, but somehow this is so much better than I ever imagined.

Except that I'm not supposed to be kissing him.

I'm supposed to be keeping things friendly so they don't get confused between us.

I pull away, breaking the kiss and leaving both of us sitting there with somewhat confused expressions on our faces.

"I'm sorry," he says.

I shake my head. "Don't be."

"Krissi..."

I don't know what he's going to say, but I'm sure I won't be able to hear it without crumbling and ending up going back on everything I promised myself when I first arrived at Obscure Academy. "I need to go," I mumble, grabbing my phone and heading towards the door.

"Krissi, we should talk about this."

"Not now." Pain lances through my heart at ignoring him. I don't want him to think the kiss was bad, that's the kind of confession that leads me to follow my heart instead of my head.

"I'm sorry. I need to go," I repeat. I need to talk to Grace, even if I already know what she's going to say. Putting some distance between me and Jeremy is almost as important as talking through how I feel.

"It's your room," he reminds me.

But it's too late, I'm out of the door and hurrying away. I don't even stop to type a message out to my friend. I'm sure she'll forgive me when I turn up at her door unannounced.

Though she may not be the best person to turn to for advice when she seems very into the idea of me dating Jeremy.

I push the thought aside and focus on putting as much distance between me and the handsome tiger shifter I abandoned in my room, all while trying to ignore the way my lips are tingling with the echo of our kiss.

There's probably no coming back from this, and I don't know how to deal with that.

10

Krissi

MUD COATS all of the rugby players from head to toe thanks to last night's rain. But that isn't enough to disguise which of them is Jeremy.

I wish it was the football team playing today, except that I know Grace would have hated that. She claims it's demoralising for us to cheer for a team that always loses.

She's not wrong. The Obscure Academy football team leaves a lot to be desired in terms of how well they can actually play, unlike both the rugby and basketball teams.

"There's no chance they're going to beat us," Grace says from beside me, her blue and white cheerleading uniform matching the rest of the team's.

"Not with the score like that," I respond, nodding to the board displaying it. The Obscure team is so ahead that there's no chance the team from Sabre Woods Academy can catch up. For a team made up of powerful big cat shifters, they haven't been tough competition.

Though the game is played by the human rules, so I don't suppose it matters much what they can shift into.

"Get in line," Zara calls. "As soon as the whistle blows, we need to be in formation for the celebration cheer."

We don't waste any time getting into position, Zara isn't one to be messed with. I'm sure she's lovely when she's relaxing, but that's not something anyone could accuse her of when she's directing the squad.

The final whistle sounds, cementing the score and the win for our rugby team.

Zara nods once and we all start moving as one. The more experienced members of the squad start doing acrobatics and starting to build a human pyramid, while the newer members like me and Grace stick to kicks and shouts. It's not an overly complicated routine, and I could do every part of it. I suspect the same is true of Grace, she's grown up cheering just like I have. But this is about trust in the rest of the team. The second and third year students have been working together for longer, the trust is there.

The two teams approach one another and start shaking hands. The whole grounds are buzzing with excited students who have come out to watch the match.

This is one of the things I like the most about cheerleading. It's fun to compete for our own trophies, but there's something completely electric about the atmosphere surrounding a game.

With the pleasantries finished, people start pouring down from the stands to join their friends.

I glance at the field, searching for Jeremy's familiar form. A small part of me wants to go over and congratulate him on a good game, but that also sort of defeats the point of me avoiding him.

Before I can make the decision, a blonde girl approaches him and waves. He doesn't seem surprised and the two of them strike up a conversation.

An uncomfortable feeling settles in my stomach as I watch them. I try to ignore it, but it only grows when she reaches out and touches his arm.

"You know who that is, right?" Jazz asks from beside me.

"No?" I turn to face my fellow cheerleader and shifter, trying my best to not seem as surprised as I am that she's there. I don't want anyone to realise how caught up in Jeremy I can be. "Who is it?"

"That's the Shifter Queen."

I blink a couple of times, trying to make her out from the distance. She doesn't look much older than I am, if at all. Though I know that's true, somehow it doesn't quite compute with the idea in my head about what the head of the shifter world should look like.

"What's she doing here?" I ask.

"She goes to Sabre Woods Academy," Jazz says. "Though I don't know what she's doing talking to Jeremy."

"He knows her," I respond without thinking about it.

"How?"

"Something about them almost being engaged at one point. I'm not really sure. He hasn't told me the whole story."

"They certainly look familiar with one another," she says. "I hope he introduces us."

Jealousy rears its ugly head within me. I know there's nothing going on between them, but I can't help but dislike it.

What do I even do about that?

Jazz disappears to go talk to someone else, probably deciding that I don't know anything about Jeremy and the blonde he's talking to.

"If you stare at them any harder, they might burst into flames," Grace says.

I let out a frustrated sigh. "I know it's stupid, but it bothers me."

"Why is it stupid? You guys kissed, and it clearly meant something to you. I bet it did to him too."

"It's stupid because I know nothing is going on with them. He told me that."

My friend raises an eyebrow. "He made sure you knew he didn't have anything going on with someone else?" Her tone suggests I should have realised how much he likes me just from that.

"Yes. He said they were friends."

"Are you trying to convince me they are, or yourself?" Grace asks.

I sigh and turn away. "It doesn't matter. He can flirt with whoever he wants."

"If that's true, then why do you look like you're about to go and scratch her eyes out?"

"That wouldn't work. She's a tiger shifter like Jeremy, she's bigger than I am in cat form."

"Who said anything about being in cat form?" Grace counters. "I was thinking you'd do it in this one."

I let out a soft snort. "I'm not exactly the eye-gouging type."

"Hmm. True. I could curse her? I can't say that pixie curses are very effective. They're more annoying really. One of the best ones makes it feel like there's a stone in your shoe, but you can never find it."

I stop in my tracks. "You're a pixie."

She grins sheepishly. "Sorry, I couldn't think of a better way of telling you. I've been trying to find the right time to drop it into conversation for a couple of weeks."

"I'm glad you feel safe enough to tell me."

A blush spreads across her cheeks. "I've never had to tell anyone before," she admits. "Most people around me just know."

"Your secret is safe with me. If it is a secret." I have to assume as much or she'd have told me already.

"I don't know," she admits. "Sometimes, I wish it

was out in the open and I didn't have to worry about it. But some people can be so distrusting of any type of fae even when there's no reason to."

"You did just say you'd curse someone to make it feel like there was a stone in their shoe," I point out.

"It's *mischief*," she stresses. "Never anything bad."

"I know." I smile reassuringly at my friend, hoping she knows that I mean what I'm saying. I don't care that she's a pixie, it doesn't change anything about her.

Besides, it's not like she's cursed me. The only problems I have are of my own making.

I glance over my shoulder to where Jeremy is still talking to the Shifter Queen.

"You know you're not going to change anything by staring at them?" Grace says. "If you don't believe that they're just friends, then call Jeremy out on it."

"I believe him about that."

"So what's the problem?"

I sigh. "I don't like how it makes me feel to see him talking to someone else like that," I admit.

"Would it be different if he was officially your boyfriend?" she asks.

"I don't know."

The look she throws me says that she doesn't believe me in the slightest.

"All right, it would be different."

"Then you know what you have to do."

She's right, and I know it. Today is only proving that more than any other that I have to do something to change the situation or I'm going to drive myself crazy in the process.

Which means I need to talk to Jeremy. Now I just have to work out what I'm going to say.

11

Jeremy

I GLANCE in the direction of the cheer squad, easily picking out Krissi from the lineup. I'm about to head over to go see her when someone clears their throat behind me.

"Have you been avoiding the palace, Jeremy?" a familiar voice asks.

"Kayra." I turn in time to be enveloped in a quick hug from the Shifter Queen. I glance around to make sure no one is paying much attention. Not that many of the Obscure Academy students around probably know who she is, but that's a good thing for her, it means she gets to just be herself without any worries about what people might think. "What are you doing here?"

"I'm here to support the Sabre Woods rugby team, and to see you. Now the team has lost, I'll have to say the second one was more my reasoning," she jokes.

I let out a low chuckle. "You'd have thought they'd play better with their Queen cheering them on."

Kayra shakes her head in amusement. "I don't think they particularly care, not with the cheerleaders you've got over there. I saw you eyeing them up."

"I'm not eyeing the cheerleaders up," I respond quickly.

"Ah, I see, then you're interested in just one of them."

I start to compose an argument in my head, but then remember who I'm talking to. "My flatmate, Krissi."

She raises an eyebrow. "Does she know that you're staring at her like you don't want there to be a field between the two of you?"

"I think so."

"Uh-oh, that doesn't sound good."

I sigh. "I think she's scared of being in a relationship."

"Then you're doing something to scare her," Kayra admonishes me. "Tell me everything."

"Everything? Don't you need to get back to running the country?"

"You and I both know I reformed that so that other people do it."

"You're not making yourself sound like a good queen," I tease.

She shrugs. "I imagine there are plenty of people who don't think I am, but I've done more for the shifter community in the past year than my mother did through her entire reign."

She isn't wrong. Her mother seemed more concerned with avoiding announcing Kayra as her heir, and trying to marry her off. I'm still not completely sure why the old queen set her sights on me as her potential son-in-law, but I'm grateful that Kayra never fell for it.

"Anyway, spill. Everything. Does she know you're interested?"

"I hope so, we kissed."

"Sober?"

"What do you take me for?"

"A twenty-year-old tiger shifter," she responds dryly.

"Yes, we were sober."

"Okay, and who started the kiss?" Kayra asks.

I rub the back of my neck nervously. "I'm not sure."

"Interesting."

"Do people normally keep track of that kind of thing? Do you know who started your first kiss with Magnus?" Is this the kind of thing girls remember? Did I ruin that for Krissi?

"He did."

"Ah." So I have ruined it.

"All right, stop feeling sorry for yourself, it doesn't matter who started it, what matters is what happened after," she says.

"Krissi ran away."

Kayra raises an eyebrow, an amused expression darting across her face. "If you're that bad of a kisser, it looks like I got off easy."

"Kissing you wouldn't be the same as kissing Krissi," I mutter.

"Oh?"

"Well, I like Krissi."

"You liked me too," she points out.

"Not the same way."

"Wow, you must really like her," Kayra says. "I'm glad, you deserve someone special."

"Thanks." Is it weird to have this conversation with someone that could have become my wife?

It's strange to think about it like that way, especially when we're both still so young. And because she has Magnus too. I like Kayra, she's a good person, but the friendship we have is nothing compared to what she has with her boyfriend.

And that's something I want for myself.

I glance back in Krissi's direction, but she's already gone.

"Can I give you some unsolicited advice?" Kayra asks.

I let out a soft snort. "If I say no, will you give it to me anyway?"

"Absolutely."

"Why even ask?" I mutter.

She ignores me and crosses her arms, giving me the sternest look she can, which is surprisingly terrifying given she's petite and blonde. "If you want things to work with Krissi, then you need to respect her wishes. If she's not ready for the two of you to have a relationship, then you need to listen to her. If you don't, you'll ruin any chance you have of making it work."

"Speaking from experience?"

"You know I am. And it worked. Magnus gave me space, and now he gets the dubious honour of escorting me to lots of balls and parties."

Despite the seriousness of the conversation, I let out a laugh. "I've seen the way he looks at you during those events, I don't think he sees it as a dubious honour."

"Hmm maybe. You know there's a ball coming up soon. You should bring Krissi, even if it's just as a friend."

"I'll ask and see what she says. I'm not even sure she believed me when I told her I knew you."

Kayra laughs. "To be fair, if some guy I barely knew told me he knew the Shifter Queen, I wouldn't believe him either."

"Is it really that unbelievable that we almost got engaged?"

She blinks a couple of times. "*Please* say that you didn't tell a girl you want to date that we were almost engaged?"

"I don't remember exactly what I said." That's a lie. I know that I told her that I was.

Kayra groans. "Jeremy, you idiot."

Have I really made that big of a mistake? Krissi didn't seem too bothered by it at the time.

"If she likes me, it'll be fine," Kayra promises, probably seeing my question in my expression. "But it means you'll have to bring her to the next ball, that way she can meet me and realise I'm not a threat."

"Were you ever a threat?"

A small smirk lifts the corners of her mouth. "To certain people."

Ah, of course. It's easy to forget that the twenty-year-old blonde in front of me has already completed one of the toughest trials known to shifters, and deposed the previous monarch.

"Anyway, I have to get going. But it was good to see you," she says. "I'll message you about the ball."

"See you later, Kayra." I wave at her as I think through the advice she's given me.

I hope I haven't messed things up too badly with Krissi. For now, I'm going to do exactly what Kayra said and respect Krissi's wishes. Maybe things will change in time, but I don't want to ruin our friendship over a relationship that may not even happen.

Krissi

I SIGH and dump my bag on the bench in front of the rows of uncomfortable fold-down seating. I hate lectures in halls like this, it's almost always hard to hear, and the seats are all connected together, meaning that the whole bench shakes if someone has a nervous twitch, making it virtually impossible to make any notes.

I glance longingly at the door, wishing I could escape and go do anything other than sit through an hour and a half of the lecturer droning on about the reasons the existence of vampires is good for the economy. The advantages of having an entire workforce that is nocturnal isn't lost on me, but it seems to be a simple concept being heavily over complicated.

"Can I sit here?"

I look up to find Jeremy standing at the end of the bench.

My mouth goes dry. I've been avoiding him ever since our kiss. "Mmhmm."

He shuffles in and sits in the seat next to me.

"I didn't realise you had this lecture." I've never seen him at it before, but then we never bothered to compare schedules. I always assumed his would be different.

"I didn't take this module last year, so I thought I would this year," he answers. "I'm starting to regret the choice."

I let out a soft snort. "You're not alone. But I know this is the kind of module that employers really like."

"Because it's imperative that we all understand the ins and outs of international economies, even if we're going into a completely unrelated field."

"That's the way the world works," I point out.

"So true."

We lapse into silence. I reach out and grab my coffee cup. I take a drink, mostly for something to do, but the sweet chai tea is a welcome distraction from Jeremy sitting beside me. I know we need to talk about what's going on between us, but it's difficult to find the right words to.

"Oh well done on the win on Wednesday," I say. "You played well."

"Thanks." He smiles reassuringly. "I was surprised, I thought the Sabre Woods team would be more of a challenge. Maybe it's the magic of being cheered by the best cheerleaders in the country." The grin he flashes me shows just how seriously he means the words.

I shake my head in bemusement. "If you say so."

"You don't think you're the best?"

"We don't have the trophy to say so."

"Isn't that because the competition isn't until next month?"

"You've got me there," I admit. "Zara's been pushing us extra hard because she thinks we're going to fail."

"That doesn't sound very inspirational."

I shrug. "That's just cheer captains for you. They can be taskmasters."

"Even more so than rugby coaches," he jokes.

A small smile tugs at the corners of my lips. "Yours doesn't seem too bad."

"He's not," he admits. "I've certainly known worse."

We lapse into silence and I glance towards the front of the lecture hall to be sure we're not in danger of getting into trouble for talking over the lecturer.

I breathe a sigh of relief as I realise he's busy talking to a small group of students.

"He never starts on time," Jeremy says, noticing where I'm looking.

"Which he somehow seems to think it's okay to run over. Doesn't he realise we have other classes to go to?" I lean back in my seat and take another sip of tea.

Jeremy chuckles. "Didn't you know? We're all supposed to act like each lecturer is the *only* one we're attending classes of."

"Eurgh, I don't have time for egos like that."

"I don't think many people do," he points out.

"Hmm."

"Are we still on for the shifting course?" he asks.

"Of course," I answer quickly.

"Oh good, because I was starting to think you were avoiding me."

The whole world fades away as his words sink in. "I sort of have," I whisper.

He grimaces, but nods understandingly. "I thought as much. Is it because of..."

"Is this the best place to talk about it?"

"Is there a better one?"

I let out a loud sigh. He's not wrong. I can't think of anywhere better. Our rooms would give us more privacy, but are also more intimate. I don't trust myself not to initiate a kiss again.

"I don't know what came over me," I admit. "I'm sorry. I shouldn't have kissed you."

"I'm not sure you can take the blame for a kiss like that."

I raise an eyebrow. "Are you saying it's your fault?"

"Well, no. I think it happened because we find each other attractive, and that's impossible to ignore sometimes."

"Isn't that a little bit cliché?" I ask.

"You've lost me."

"The cheerleader and the jock? We're not exactly breaking the mould in terms of pairings."

A soft snort escapes from Jeremy. "You're not wrong there. But clichés exist for a reason. I choose to look at it as that we've got something in common and that helps drive the attraction."

"Hmm."

"Are you disputing the theory, or whether you're attracted to me?" The boyish grin spreading across his face reveals the slight tease behind his words.

"Neither."

"Then you're going to have to fill me in," he says. "I'm smart, but I'm not *that* smart."

I let out a loud sigh and check the front of the room again. The last thing I want is for our conversation to end up stopped before we're ready for it to be. I may have been avoiding it as much as possible in the last few days, but I don't want anything hanging in the air between us now we've got it out in the open.

"It's just that when I came here, I promised that I'd focus on my studies and on cheering, and that I wouldn't let myself get distracted by dating."

"Promised who? You never mentioned your parents being strict like that."

"They're not. I promised myself."

"I see."

"So now I have to focus on what I promised and not get distracted."

"You know, there's one way you can try and get me out of your system." The impish grin on his face leaves absolutely no doubt as to what he's implying.

"We're not doing that," I respond hastily.

He shrugs. "Just a suggestion."

He doesn't seem all that bothered by my shut down, which bothers me, though I can't quite pinpoint why.

I sigh. "I just don't think it would work. I know what I'm like."

"I assumed as much."

Oh, okay. So it's not that he doesn't want to sleep with me. Just that he doesn't think we can end up in bed together in a casual setting. Good to know. Especially that he's on the same page as me.

"So what do we do now?" he asks. "Considering we live together, I'd much rather we moved on from you avoiding me."

I sigh. "I'd like that too."

"Okay, so friends?"

"We're already friends," I point out.

"Friends who have kissed."

"I can go back to the flat and get Essie to kiss me too if you want? That way I've kissed two of my friends."

He raises an eyebrow. "Why Essie?"

"She's mentioned I'm her type a couple of times," I say offhandedly.

"Wait, Essie's gay?"

"Bi. Were you not paying any attention during the first week?"

"I was distracted by a beautiful leopard shifter," he mutters.

A furious blush rises to my cheeks. "You can't say stuff like that, we're friends, remember?"

"Aren't friends allowed to tell other friends they look good?"

Men. I swear they can be so clueless sometimes. "Not when they're thinking about kissing them, no."

"The rules are confusing."

"They're there for a reason."

He chuckles. "All right. We'll be friends. No kissing. No thinking about kissing. Nothing. Do we have a deal?" He holds out his hand for me to shake.

I throw him an incredulous look. "Do you really want to shake on this?"

"Well we can't seal the deal with a kiss," he quips.

I shake my head in bemusement. "Fine."

I take his hand in mine and give it a firm shake. He tightens his grip ever so slightly and looks me dead in the eyes.

"The rules go for you too," he reminds me. "No thinking about kissing me."

The moment his words register, my gaze flicks down to his lips and the echo of the way they felt against mine tingles through me.

I swallow hard. "Deal."

"It's been a pleasure doing business with you, Krissi." He lets go of my hand.

"Likewise," I mumble.

The lecturer finally calls for everyone's attention,

which is a good thing given the racing thoughts in my head.

I lean back in my seat.

Why can't I shake the feeling that I've made a terrible mistake?

Krissi

EVERY PART of my body aches from the almost constant practice Zara has been encouraging us to do. I roll my head around, cracking my neck in the process.

It doesn't relieve the tension building within me. A hot shower and a good night's sleep will probably do the trick.

I can probably add a shift into the mix. My room isn't big enough for me to do much, but I don't think I have the energy for more than a quick shift and a collapse.

I slide my key into the flat lock and open it up for

myself, stepping inside. My stomach rumbles as the smell of something tasty comes from the kitchen. I better go make myself some food before I go collapse, or I'm going to wake up starving and grumpy because of it. Most people don't believe I'm capable of being that way, but that's because I'm careful not to let myself go too long without a meal in the first place.

I push open the kitchen door and dump my gym bag on the bench.

Bernie turns around to see who has come in, and her eyebrows raise as she catches sight of me still wearing my white and blue cheerleading outfit. "Isn't it a little late to be getting in from practice?"

I sigh. "Don't get me started. I've cheered for as long as I can remember, and I don't think I've ever had a coach or captain push me as hard as Zara is. Now I'm tired and hungry."

"I'm not surprised. Do you want some of this?" she asks, gesturing towards the pan. "It's nothing fancy, just some tomato pasta."

"If you don't mind, it smells really good."

"Sure, I'll take some out before I put the blood in," Bernie responds.

I don't do very well at covering my shock. "You put your blood in pasta?"

She lets out a loud sigh. "Not by choice. I'd rather

not put it in anything." She pulls out a second bowl and scoops some of the pasta into it before holding it out to me. "Here you go."

"Thanks, Bernie. You don't know how much I appreciate this."

"It's no bother. You can make me a meal some-time if you want to."

"I will," I promise. I open my cupboard and grab my spoon and head back to the table. I dig in, discovering that it tastes just as good as it smells. I don't know who taught Bernie to cook, but it's good.

Bernie heads to the fridge and pulls out a sealed container.

I don't need to ask to know what's inside it. I've lived with her long enough to be able to recognise the blood pouches she needs to consume in order to survive.

"Oh, I didn't think to check, you're okay eating vegetarian, right?" she asks, clearly trying to put off opening the blood.

I nod. "It won't sit well with me if I eat it while I'm shifted, but I can eat vegetarian when I'm in my human form and it won't cause me any problems. And it's tasty to have sometimes too. But are you really adding blood to vegetarian food?"

She wrinkles her nose. "I was vegetarian before I was turned," she admits.

My eyebrows shoot up. "I didn't realise you were a turned vampire."

"You had no reason to," she assures me. "It doesn't really make much difference at this point in my life. Only later down the line."

Ah. Right. Turned vampires are technically dead and can't reproduce as a result. I've heard rumours that there are scientists working on it, but I'm not sure how close they are to finding a solution.

"Is that why you don't like drinking blood now?" I ask.

"I don't know," she admits. "I never really liked the taste of meat, so I guess it makes sense that I don't like the taste of blood. That's why I try to add it to food, but that doesn't really work either."

"Have you ever asked another vampire about it?" I take another bite of my pasta, feeling a little better now I'm getting food in my system.

"Actually, no. I didn't want to come across as a bad vampire."

"I don't think you're a bad vampire. You drink the blood anyway."

Bernie grimaces. "Yes. But only because I fear the consequences if I don't." With that, she rips the seal off the blood and stares at it. "I really don't want to ruin the pasta by adding it."

"You could drink it down really fast and then eat to get rid of the taste?" I suggest.

Bernie sighs. "I'm going to have to. Do you mind?"

"Of course not Be my guest." I don't want to make her feel any more uncomfortable about her blood consumption than she has to, especially when she's been kind enough to share her meal with me.

She takes a deep breath and gulps it down, barely stopping once she's gotten started. She scrunches up the empty packet and throws it towards the bin. She covers her hand with her mouth and doesn't say anything while breathing in and out rapidly. Her pale skin grows even paler still, and I start to wonder about whether I need to call for medical attention.

"That was disgusting," she mutters.

"I'm sorry you have to do that."

"It's not your fault. Unless you're trying to tell me that you're secretly the old man who turned me."

"Not last time I checked," I attempt to joke, but really I'm just feeling a little sad for her.

She loads up her plate and comes to join me. "Thank you for being with me when I drank," she says. "It actually helps to have someone around."

"I didn't really do anything."

"I know. But I guess it just feels like moral support." She piles up her spoon with pasta and a more blissful expression crosses her face once the taste hits her tongue.

"If you ever need more of it, you can come find me," I promise. "But maybe you should think about asking one of the other vampires for some advice. Maybe someone else who has been turned will be able to help you?" I hope I'm not overstepping by suggesting it. I'm not as close to her as Essie is, but I feel like we're good enough friends for me to say it.

She offers me a genuine smile. "I think I'm going to. Every time I have to drink blood, I try to convince myself that it's not that bad and I need to get past it. But I can't do this for the rest of my life."

"Are there no blood substitutes available?"

"There's a rumour that there was someone making synthetic stuff while there was that blood drought in the City of Blood a couple of years ago, but it doesn't seem to have hit the main market yet."

"That's a shame, it would be good if you could get hold of some."

"I know. But it probably has to go through a load of testing before it's allowed to be sold to the public. It might not be any better, but I'm going to hold onto the hope that it will be."

"I do too." Completely for her sake, but the words are true. I suspect there are a lot of people who would be happier to have it as an option.

We finish our food while chatting amicably about various parts of life at the academy, and I end up feeling closer to Bernie than I have before. Which is a good thing. Spending time with her is harder than with the others because of the whole vampires-being-allergic-to-the-sun-in-a-big way thing. Honestly, the more I learn about them, the more relieved I am to be a shifter. Vampire life sounds very restricting.

A large yawn escapes me and I cover my mouth with my hand. "I'm sorry, it's been a long day."

"That's okay, I need to get going to one of my lectures anyway. You'd think they'd be more lenient on vampire students, but we only have a few hours to cram our classes into."

"They should start doing some remote teaching so you don't have to leave your dorms for it," I point out.

"I think they do in the summer terms when the sun barely goes away."

"Ah, that makes sense." And must be awful for the poor vampires. I get to my feet and hold out my hand for her dish. "I'll wash up while you get going. It's only fair when you cooked."

"Thanks, Krissi."

"No problem."

We share a quick smile and she hands it over,

getting up and heading for the door. "I'll let you know how I get on with the vampires."

"I'd like that." I wave goodbye to her and focus on washing things quickly so I can get my shower and head to bed. I already feel a little bit better, but I know it's only temporary. I don't know how I'm going to manage with another week of late-night practices, especially when I have the shifter course coming up with Jeremy. But I'll manage, and it'll all be worth it when we lift the cheerleading trophy, I'm sure of it.

Krissi

I TUG on the strap of my workout shirt, already worrying that I'm wearing the wrong thing. Which is ridiculous when I'm not even going to be in human form for the rest of the afternoon.

"Hey," Jeremy says, waving at me as he approaches.

My traitorous heart flutters at the sight of him. We're supposed to be friends, and today is going to prove it, but I'm not sure how well I'm going to cope with that when I'm already having a reaction to him and we haven't even said much yet.

It'll be easier once we're shifted.

I hope.

"Hey," I return.

"Are you ready?"

I chew on my bottom lip and his gaze briefly flicks down to them before he clears his throat and looks away.

This is getting harder by the moment.

"Is it bad if I say no?"

He shakes his head. "Have you ever been around this many big cat shifters before?" he asks.

"Only on the Sabre Woods Academy open day," I admit. "I hated it. I felt like such a fraud when they started showing off their shifter forms and I just wanted to stay human."

"Is that why you really didn't go there? I know you said you thought the curriculum here is better."

"The range of classes is the main thing behind my decision," I admit. "But I can't pretend that the way I felt at Sabre Woods wasn't a factor, but I think it's more than that."

He nods and I know he understands. He's spent time at the big cat academy, even if it wasn't as a student, and even if he hadn't, he's spent time at the shifter court, which I imagine is so much worse.

"Shall we go inside?" he asks, gesturing towards the gate that leads into the compound where we'll be doing our training.

"We should if we don't want to be late." I don't want to make a bad impression, especially when it's bad enough that I'm going to have to shift. I know that I'm going to appear terribly incompetent when I do. After all, what kind of eighteen-year-old shifter doesn't have control of her paws?

Jeremy gestures for me to go first and moves his other hand as if he's going to place it on the small of my back before changing his mind.

Disappointment wells up within me at the missing touch, and I have to remind myself that we're friends, nothing more. It's reassuring to know he's struggling a little bit with it too, but does that mean we're kidding ourselves about whether we can do this?

Grace's comment about him still being a distraction even if I don't want him to be springs to mind.

Several other students I recognise mill around the courtyard, along with some I don't. I frown. I know the academy is bigger than the people I know, but I don't even recognise them in passing, which is a little confusing.

A middle-aged man steps forward and whistles for our attention. "Good afternoon, everyone. Welcome to Shifter Agility training. Today's course is aimed at big cat shifters, if you are a different kind of shifter, then I highly advise that you change to a different date. There will be things on this course that you won't be able to achieve."

A small murmur goes through the assembled students, probably as people try to work out what the different parts of the course might be.

Instead of making me more intrigued by what's to come, I get more nervous. I take a step back, bringing me flush against Jeremy's chest and causing me to stumble.

A girl to the left of us gives a small laugh, but I ignore her as Jeremy reaches out to help steady me.

"You'll be okay," he promises, and from his tone, I can tell that he believes it's true.

"You've seen me shifted," I point out in a whisper. "How can you say it's going to be okay?"

"You were drunk then."

"Trust me when I say I'm not much better at it when I'm sober." Much to the annoyance of just about everyone in my life.

"Krissi," he says firmly. "You can do this. And I'm not going to leave you behind, I'll help you every step of the way."

A vague memory of his shifted form flits through my mind. While I know he shifted and helped me when I was foolish enough to change forms in the street, I don't really remember much of what he actually looks like when he's a tiger.

"All right, put your belongings in the lockers over there and shift," the instructor calls.

I chew on my bottom lip as I follow Jeremy over to the lockers in question. Why am I doing this? It's such a bad idea and I'm only going to end up embarrassing myself in front of someone I like.

As a friend. Like as a friend.

I don't think I'm fooling anyone, including myself any longer.

I grab a hair tie from my bag and put my hair into a high ponytail.

Jeremy raises an eyebrow. "Why are you doing that if you're going to shift?"

I frown, realising that he has a point. "I don't know, but we're about to go on an obstacle course, it feels like the right kind of thing to do if I want to get ready."

To my surprise, he just nods, seeming to understand the logic. "Anything that helps."

"Precisely." He's going to understand just how important that is soon. I set the code on my locker and turn to face Jeremy. "I guess we have to shift now."

"Want me to go first?" he offers.

"Yes." The admission is out of my mouth before I can think twice about it, but it's the truth. I think I'll feel better if I can see his form while I'm not worrying about my own.

In the blink of an eye, the tall auburn-haired guy in front of me is replaced by a huge tiger. His dark orange fur suits him, and the black stripes only add to the illusion of power and grace.

Without thinking about it, I reach out and place my hand on his head. Realising how rude it is of me to touch him like this, I snatch my hand back.

Jeremy is having none of it and steps forward to press his head against my hand.

Spurred on by his permission, I sink my fingers into his thick fur. He lets out a loud rumbling purr that makes me feel all warm and fuzzy inside. I know he's still just Jeremy, but something about having his tiger's approval feels special.

I shake my head and pull myself out of the tiger-induced daze. Most of the other students have already shifted, which means it's time for me to do the same, even if it'll probably end badly for me.

I close my eyes and pull on the thread of magic within me that will change me into a leopard. Despite having been a shifter my entire life, I'm still not sure exactly how the magic works, just that it does.

My body morphs just as quickly as Jeremy's did, though my leopard form is smaller than his tiger one. I suppose that makes sense given that I'm smaller as a human too.

Despite my reservations about shifting, there's something undeniably freeing about being in this form. I think it's the way the world feels. It's different, full of adventure and promise. I should shift more often, but for obvious reasons, I try to avoid it.

Jeremy must catch onto the drift of my thoughts as he steps forward and pushes his head against the side of my neck in a show of support.

Or affection. But it's best if I don't dwell on that part.

"I see you're all shifted now," the instructor calls, still as a human. But now I'm in my animal form I can sense the lion sleeping within him and longing to run free with the feline shifters assembled. "You can enter the course now. Each of the obstacles is designed in order to test and strengthen your skills as a feline shifter."

Or reveal the lack of skills in my case.

Most of the others rush to the entrance, but I hang back, too nervous to be able to be the first one through.

Jeremy stays with me, only moving when it becomes clear that we're going to be the last ones. Another surge of affection floods through me. He's doing it on purpose so I don't feel like anyone else is watching me.

Knowing he's there to help gives me the confidence I need to put one paw in front of the other. This is going to go badly, but at least I have someone looking after me while it does.

Jeremy

Even though she can't say anything, I can feel the apprehension coming from Krissi in waves. I wish I could do more to help her than off a bit of moral support, but that seems to be the best I can muster right now.

I put one paw in front of the other, doing my best to keep an eye on the leopard shifter beside me. Other than the fact she looks like she's about to fall over, she's beautiful, and certainly has the grace that comes with being a big cat shifter.

The problems start when she tries to move.

I let out a low rumble to let her know that I'm

still within touching distance if anything goes wrong.

She startles and swings her head around in my direction. Even in leopard form, I can see her eyes going wide and panic setting in. She isn't going to be able to move a muscle if she carries on like this. Maybe suggesting we did the class together was a mistake.

I glance around to make sure no one is paying us any attention and pull my human form to the front. I balance precariously on the log, not quite as secure now I'm wearing shoes.

She cocks her head to the side and studies me, as if surprised to find me in human form. She eyes the distance between us as if to decide whether she's going to join me.

"I'll come to you," I promise, though now I look at the gap, I'm not sure I'll be able to manage. As a tiger, it would be easy, but I don't think she'll react well if I jump over there in my bigger form.

She jerks her head to the side as if shaking it.

I pause, unsure what she's trying to say. This is part of the problem of being in shifter form. Unless you know the other person well enough to be able to sense what they're trying to say, it's virtually impossible to communicate. I think I can probably get to that place with Krissi at some point in the future, but right now, we haven't known one another long enough.

To my surprise, she doesn't jump in her leopard form. Instead, she also shifts back to human and then takes a run up and flips herself over and onto the log next to me, balancing with all the grace and ease she's missing in her leopard form.

"You okay?" I ask her.

She grimaces. "Would you believe me if I said yes?"

I shake my head. "I have eyes."

"Then no, I'm not. I know this is supposed to help, but all it's doing is making me constantly worry about what will happen if I fall off."

"That won't happen."

She raises an eyebrow, clearly aware that I'm lying to her. I suppose that's better than her thinking that she's great at this kind of thing.

Krissi sighs and rubs a hand over her face. "It's okay, I just need to find the courage to carry on with this and not worry about making a fool out of myself." She looks over to where two of the others are jumping between posts, barely seeming to stop to look where they're going.

Despite knowing it isn't the best for us if we want to keep our friendship just that, I reach out and touch her arm gently. "You can do it," I assure her. "And I'll be here the whole time."

She smiles weakly. "I know you will."

"But it's not enough?"

She glances at her feet but not quickly enough to hide the furious blush spreading across her face. "I don't want you to think badly of me when I fail."

It takes a moment for the words to sink in, but once they do, I reach out and pull her to me. She wraps her arms around my waist and leans her head against my shoulder. I breathe her in, my sense of smell heightened thanks to the recent shift.

A flowery scent comes from her, which I assume must be her shampoo, it's pleasant and makes me want to get to know it better.

"I promise that no matter what happens, I'm not going to judge you for it," I say, meaning every word. "You could fall off every obstacle from here until the end, and I'll still be there to cheer you on."

"I thought cheering was my job," she mumbles.

I chuckle, causing a small sigh to come from Krissi, though I don't think it's a bad one. More a sigh of contentment.

My tiger is ready to come out and start protecting her from anyone who makes her feel bad about her poor shifting skills. I'm of half a mind to let it happen.

"Sometimes it needs to come from someone else or it doesn't count as cheering," I point out. "So when I'm following you around the course, you can know that in my head, I'm chanting your name over and over again."

She half pulls out of our embrace and frowns at me. "You realise that sounds really creepy, right?"

"Only if you're not into it."

She chuckles. "You've got me there, I actually thought it was cute."

"Good to know." And that she doesn't seem to be thinking of me in *just friends* terms anymore. If she ever really has.

No. I can't think like that. She's made it clear that she doesn't want to be anything more than friends and I need to accept that. Even if I hope there's still a chance for us, it needs to be on her terms.

I study the gorgeous brunette in front of me, and what strikes me the most is how different I feel now than when I was in this position with Kayra. She told me she just wanted us to be friends and I accepted it without question and never really thought about the chance of more. But with Krissi, the feelings haven't gone away just because she says she wants us to be friends.

I push the thoughts to the side. There's no use dwelling on them when they won't change anything anyway. And now really isn't the time to be thinking about anything other than getting Krissi to the end of the course.

She steps back and I immediately feel her loss.

"I'm ready," she says. "But you have to promise to catch me if I fall."

"I'll promise that I'll try," I counter. "Whether I succeed is another matter."

"That's fair." She closes her eyes and before her words have even fully registered, she's back in her leopard form.

I stare at her for a moment, lost in how beautiful she is. A small part of me wants to reach out and put my hand in her fur the same way she did to me, but I don't dare to unless she initiates.

Pulling myself out of it, I tug my own big cat to the surface and transform into my tiger form. I'm bigger than she is, but the difference isn't as big as I expected it to be.

I gesture with my head towards the next obstacle, which appears to be a set of stones over a fake river. I can already see what's going to happen, but luckily, I like the water.

Krissi leaps towards the first stone, landing on it in the exact position she's supposed to. She glances back over her shoulder, gleaming yellow eyes locking onto mine.

I don't need to be able to understand her to know what she's feeling.

Surprise.

I nod my large head, encouraging her to continue.

She jumps again, managing to stay on the stones for a second time. I can almost feel her excitement from here.

I know there's a good chance this isn't going to last, but Krissi doesn't seem like the kind of person who will let a little bit of failure get her down. She'll be focusing on what she actually managed to achieve more than what she didn't.

And if she struggles with that, I'll be there to remind her of just how amazing she is.

16

Krissi

GIDDY NERVES FILL me as we walk into the room full of cheerleaders. There's nothing like competition day, even if I'm not convinced we have what it takes to actually win.

Grace hooks her arm through mine. "It feels different, doesn't it?" she asks.

"What does?"

"Walking in here when we know we'll be competing against people we previously competed with. There are some people I'm looking forward to finally being able to beat, but there are others who I'm sad at the thought of having to make fail."

"I know what you mean. But I'm still excited."

"Same. I think we have a good chance at winning."

"You do?"

She nods. "With how hard Zara's been drilling us, how can we not? You've got to think like a winner to be a winner, Krissi."

"If you say so."

"Well if you can't believe it yourself, then I'll have to believe it for you." She closes her eyes. "Krissi is a winner, Krissi is a winner," she mutters to herself.

I bat her on the arm. "You can stop that now."

"Fine, but only if you start having more faith in the team," she counters. "Though maybe it doesn't matter." Her lips curl into a smile.

"What?"

"Look." She nods in the direction of a group of people I recognise.

My breathing hitches as I recognise the tall, auburn-haired guy at the centre of the group.

"So I suppose the question is whether some of your flatmates came because Jeremy asked them to, or did Jeremy come because they did?" Grace muses.

"I don't think it matters," I admit, unable to take my eyes off my friends.

"Come on, let's go say hi."

"Zara..."

"Isn't paying any attention to us, she's too busy throwing down with the other captain." She gestures to where that does seem to be taking place while dragging me towards the others.

I don't mind too much, I'm glad they've come to support us, a lot of people don't necessarily see cheering as something to watch as a spectator.

"Hey, guys," Grace says, waving. "I didn't realise you were coming, Krissi didn't tell me."

"That's because we didn't tell Krissi," Mickie responds. "It was a last-minute thing. Jeremy asked us to come." She throws him a look that I don't think he notices.

But I do. And I know what it means.

"Hey." I give him a half-wave.

Grace lets go of my other arm and I'm dimly aware of her moving my other flatmates away from us, leaving me and Jeremy in reasonable privacy.

"I hope you don't mind, I thought you'd want the support."

I fiddle with a strand of hair, feeling more nervous than before, but I'm not too sure exactly what's causing it. "Thank you, it's nice. I didn't even realise you were coming."

"I should have checked it was okay."

I shake my head. "It's fine. I watch your games all

the time," I remind him. "It's nice to think you're watching me compete in my sport."

"That's what I thought. Then Mickie heard I was coming and she gave me this look."

I let out a light laugh. "I know the one you mean."

"And then she insisted on coming along with me and invited the others."

"Ah, so it wasn't quite that you invited them."

"I think she's trying to make sure we don't do anything she doesn't approve of," he agrees.

"Right, because she thinks I'm leading you on." The words are out before I can think twice about them. But now they're out, I might as well double down on them. "Am I? I don't mean to be, and if I am..."

Jeremy leans in, closing the gap between us. It isn't uncomfortable, quite the opposite. "I don't think you're leading me on," he assures me. "You've told me where you stand."

"There's a but."

"There is," he agrees. "I wasn't going to say anything about it."

"But now we're talking," I finish for him.

"Exactly. Now we're talking." He takes a deep breath. "I don't think I can just be your friend, Krissi. I want to be at these events without people giving me side looks and asking what it means."

My breathing quickens and I realise as I hear him saying it that I want that too. I've been so determined to avoid the distraction otherwise known as Jeremy, that I've managed to turn something that could be a supportive relationship into something keeping me from achieving what I came here to do because it's all I'm able to think about.

"I..."

"We have to go." Grace tugs on my arm.

"But..." I glance at Jeremy, wanting to finish what I was about to tell him.

"Zara's on a warpath," Grace mutters.

"We can talk later," Jeremy assures me. "Go win a trophy first."

I think about arguing, but end up nodding instead. It's fine to prioritise. He's not going to change his mind about his feelings for me in the next half an hour.

"Did I just interrupt something?" Grace asks.

"You know you did," I mutter.

"Sorry, but Zara is fuming, I didn't want her to take it out on you."

I sigh. "It's okay. I'll deal with it after." I sound more confident than I feel.

I glance over my shoulder and back at Jeremy who smiles and waves at me. Instead of feeling jittery and distracted, I feel more grounded knowing someone is watching who wants me to succeed more than anything.

"You seem different," Grace says.

"I think I finally decided what to do about Jeremy," I admit.

"Ah. Break his heart or jump his bones?"

"Neither." Though the latter is an appealing suggestion, not that I'm about to tell the mischievous pixie about that.

"Right, well you can jump his bones after we've performed."

"I didn't say that's what I was going to do."

"Then stop biting your lip as if you're thinking about what he looks like naked."

"What? I'm not doing either of those things." Though actually, I am biting my lip.

"Mmhmm."

Our conversation is cut short when we reach the rest of our team and find Zara pacing back and forth looking as if she's about to hurt someone.

It seems Grace made the right decision in dragging me back over here. Zara is stern at the best of times, but it seems like she's in an even stricter mood than normal.

"What happened?" I ask Jazz.

The other shifter shrugs. "As far as we can tell

one of the other captains taunted her because she fell last year."

"Ouch, not good." I can only imagine how hard that has to be for Zara.

"Just another reason to win," Jazz responds.

"I thought we were supposed to say that winning doesn't matter and it's the taking part that counts," I say.

Jazz snorts. "I don't know what kind of cheer captains you've been working under before, but I don't think any of the ones I've known have ever been about anything other than winning."

"Fair point," I murmur.

"All right, team, listen up," Zara calls.

We all fall silent and turn to face her. It's impossible to miss the stress on her face. She wants this, and that's why we're going to make it happen.

"It's a tough competition today. Some of the other teams we're up against have several past wins under their belts. But if we do our routine exactly the way we've practised it, then we're going to be able to make this happen. Hands in."

Zara holds out her hand and waits for all of us to follow suit, feeling more like a team than ever. And this is the moment we get to prove it.

17

Jeremy

THE MORE TEAMS take to the floor, the more nervous I am about the Obscure Academy cheer squad's chances of winning. I've watched them from a distance several times, and seen them cheering us on at matches, so I know they're good, but are they *this* good?

Up until now, I've never really considered whether there's more to cheerleading than just what they do to support the sports team playing, but it turns out that there is.

A lot more.

"How have we not been to one of these before?"

Dylan asks, putting an arm around Cyprus.

"Is it the short skirts or the women who are well out of your league that you're admiring the most?" The necromancer answers.

Dylan chuckles. "Both."

"Are we sure Krissi does this?" Cyprus asks. "She seems more of the sweet and innocent type."

I raise an eyebrow. "You don't think she can be sweet and a cheerleader?"

"I don't know, it just doesn't seem like her thing."

"Then you're about to be proved very wrong." I nod towards the staging area where the Obscure Academy team is coming out onto the floor.

It only takes me a few moments to spot Krissi among them.

Cyprus whistles. "Krissi is secret hot."

Michaela leans forwards and bats him. "Don't talk about your flatmate like that."

"I'm not lying," Cyprus counters.

"He's not," Essie agrees. "Krissi is hot. But he should maybe have realised that already."

A low growl escapes me without me meaning it to and my flatmates turn their attention to me.

"Sorry," I mutter.

"All right, no talking about how hot Krissi is," Cyprus promises.

"I didn't mean..."

Michaela puts a hand on my shoulder to stop me from speaking. "Just take the win," she says softly.

I nod, knowing she's right.

The music starts, and my attention is soon captured by the squad on the performance floor. While the odd part of their routine is familiar, the majority of it is nothing like when they cheer for the rugby team.

Several people go flying into the air, spinning and twisting not unlike how Krissi did while we were at the shifter assault course.

Without even meaning it to happen, my gaze focuses on her. Despite knowing she's capable of them, she doesn't seem to be taking part in any of the more dangerous moves, though I have no idea why that might be. Perhaps it's to do with how long she's been on the squad. I can ask her about it later.

No one watching would have any idea that she struggles with her shifted form. Every move she makes it perfectly balanced and in time with both the music, and the rest of the squad. It's amazing to watch, and I find myself glued to the edge of my seat.

"Is it a winning routine?" Essie asks from behind me.

I can almost hear Michaela shrug in response. "I don't know enough about it," she admits. "But aren't we supposed to be recording some of this for Bernie?"

"Oh, right. I promised her I would. I think she's been having some late-night dinners with Krissi when she gets in from practice."

I didn't realise that, but it makes sense with Bernie's nocturnal hours and Krissi's late-night training.

The audience cheers as the team makes a particularly impressive looking move that includes one of the guys throwing a cheerleader up into the air and then catching her. I may want to support Krissi at events like this, but I don't know how I'm going to be able to if she's the one getting thrown up into the air like that. I know cats are supposed to land on their feet, but I've seen evidence that this one doesn't.

As if the routine senses what I'm most nervous about, Krissi springs into a backflip, becoming barely more than a blur of blue and white.

My heart pounds as I watch and I'm unable to tear my eyes away. I've seen her perform acrobatics like this multiple times, and yet I'm still worried she's going to get hurt.

She's caught moments later by one of the others and set on her feet again.

The audience makes a loud noise again, though I

don't think it's to do with Krissi's move, she still seems to be on the outside of the group. I'm sure that will change as they compete more and Zara realises the talent the leopard shifter has. I've known Zara long enough to know she's a hard taskmaster, but talent matters to her, and Krissi's won't go unnoticed.

The music comes to an end and the team all stills as one. They form two neat rows and bow to the judges.

"Do you think they did enough to win?" Michaela asks.

"I honestly have no idea," I admit. "All of this is completely new to me."

"I thought you were supposed to know about all of this sports stuff." She waves her hand towards the staging area.

"Within reason," I point out. "But I had no idea this is what Krissi meant when she talked about competitive cheering, this is the first time I've been to an event."

"Well that's no use," Michaela mutters.

"Especially because the only cheerleader we know that we can ask is biased. Krissi's never going to say that was a winning routine, even if it is," Essie adds.

"I should go find her," I say, getting to my feet and

walking off before either of them can stop me. It may not be the best idea I've ever had, but we were about to have an important conversation before Grace dragged her away, I'd like to get back to that and find out if Krissi is going to say what I hope she will.

Krissi

THE BUZZ of performing bounces around my system even though we've been off stage for twenty minutes and have fully been through our cool down routine. I'm not sure if the others feel it the same way I do, but it's almost more exhilarating than how it feels after a shift.

Without the embarrassment of nearly having fallen over. I don't need anyone to tell me that I executed all of my moves flawlessly, I'm aware that I did.

I scan the crowd for Jeremy before I even realise what I'm doing, and not just because we still have to talk. I want to see him and hear what he thinks about our performance. I didn't realise I cared as much as I do until this moment, but his support means a lot to me and I want more of it.

Grace is right, I'm completely distracted by Jeremy, even if I haven't wanted to admit it. All I have to do now is decide how to undo the damage I've already done by telling him I don't want to be anything more than friends.

Mickie waves to me from across the room, and relief fills me that they're still here, I take a step towards my flatmates, only for Grace to catch my arm.

I glance at her, but she shakes her head.

"Not yet," she says.

"But..."

"There are more important things than your love life going on right now."

"That's not what you've been saying for months," I mutter.

Grace chuckles. "And you've been ignoring me for months. Now you need to ignore me for a few more minutes while they announce the winners. It'll look bad if we're all on the stage and you're not."

"Are they ready to announce it already?"

She nods. "We were late in the running order. The last team ended their performance just before we came out of the cooldown room. Zara told us all this, were you paying any attention?"

I groan and rub my forehead. "I'm so distracted."

"Mmhmm. Ignoring the fact you have a monster-sized crush on Jeremy will do that."

"I can't wait for you to find someone and end up having to eat some of your own words."

Grace's lips twist into a small smile. "Not going to happen."

"Because you don't want to be distracted by romance?"

"Not at all. It isn't going to happen, because I'm not an idiot like you."

A small snort escapes me. "You're going to have to eat your words about that." I link my arm through hers and follow the others towards the backstage area.

"Pixies don't eat their words."

I raise an eyebrow, but don't argue with her. She's going to find out how hard it is to avoid situations like this at some point. I hope I'm around to point out how obvious she's being with whoever it is in retaliation to the way she's been making it obvious to me that I like Jeremy.

Zara paces up and down in front of us all, clearly nervous about the results. Maybe she knows something about how all of the other teams have performed. I can't say that I've been paying much attention, which I know isn't a good thing to admit.

"How long do we have to wait?" I ask.

"They're about to start the announcement," Jazz says from next to us, pointing at the scoreboard in front of us.

"Do we find out whether we've won before the audience do?" There aren't a huge amount of people here, but I still don't want to be too surprised.

She shakes her head. "They'll announce ten through four here, then tell the three teams who are at the top to go out onto the stage."

So we'll know within a few minutes if we're going to get a trophy. A small part of me knows that any of the top three positions are good because it means we get to move onto the next round of the competition, but I want to win. First place means more to me personally, and from the way she's acting, I suspect it does for Zara too.

Academy and university names start flashing up on the screen, starting with the bottom one. The whole room falls silent despite the dozens of people within it, and I can feel my heart pounding with nerves.

I can't tear my eyes away as the next few team names pop up, and the closer it gets to the top, the more I worry that we haven't managed to place at all.

It's not how it works, and that I'm being irrational, but I can't help it.

My whole body is jittering with nerves.

"We could power the lights with your nervous energy," Grace mutters to me.

"How are you staying so calm?" I respond.

"Denial."

I let out a soft snort.

The screen updates, revealing the team that's come in fourth. I stare at it for a few minutes, barely registering that it's not ours next to it.

It updates again, revealing the top three teams, with *Obscure Academy* right up there.

Jazz lets out a little squeal, but Zara's cool and collected stare shuts it down.

"It's too early to celebrate yet," Zara says to us all. "We don't know which position we've come in."

"But we're through to the next round, right?" one of the others asks.

Our captain nods, but we're ushered into the staging area before she can say anything else.

The other two teams come with us, but I don't pay any attention to them as I stand between Grace and Jazz as part of our team line. The lights are too bright for me to find my flatmates, but knowing they're watching reassures me, even if I didn't think it would.

I force a smile onto my face, knowing that it's important that we present ourselves well, especially if we don't end up winning the first place trophy.

"I'm sure you're all excited to find out which of our teams the judges have awarded full place to," the presenter says. "But a big congratulations to all of the cheer squads on the stage at the moment for making it through to the next round."

Applause and shouts come from the assembled audience as they celebrate for us. I find my smile getting bigger and becoming easier to maintain as the energy in the room starts to affect me.

"I don't want to keep you waiting any longer," the presenter says. "In third place, we have the lovely ladies from Queen Elizabeth's Academy."

A shrill scream goes up from the only all-female team on the stage and they start jumping up and down.

The captain steps forward to receive the bronze trophy, and I know there'll be medals waiting off stage for the individual team members.

My stomach starts tying itself up in knots at the realisation that we might have won after all. I know our routine was good, but I didn't see the other team perform, so it's hard to know which way it's going to go.

"And now, your winners for today's competition," the presenter says.

"Come on, come on, come on," Grace whispers from beside me, her eyes squeezed shut. I don't think I've ever seen her so desperate for anything.

"The winner is Hexington Academy," he calls.

The other team explodes into excited screams.

Disappointment wells up within me. Somehow, coming second is worse than coming third, and I have no explanation about why.

"Which means our second-place team is from Obscure Academy," the presenter says, gesturing to us.

I cheer along with the rest of the squad, but I can hear that they feel the same way I do.

Zara manages to put a smile on her face long enough to step forward and accept the trophy graciously before the presenter turns to the winning captain.

"We'll win next time," Jazz assures Zara.

Our captain smiles, but it doesn't quite reach her eyes. "We'll try."

No doubt cheer practice is about to get a whole lot harder.

Krissi

As soon as it's possible to do so, I make my excuses to leave the other team members and head back to my flat. I need to talk to Jeremy before I lose my nerve and end up regretting it.

I push the kitchen door open, summoned by the raucous laughter coming from inside.

"Hey, Krissi, congrats," Mickie says. "Are you coming out with us?" She gestures to the table littered with half-full cups of booze and a seemingly forgotten card game. They haven't wasted any time since getting back from the competition.

I shake my head. "I just need to sleep," I admit. "But I was actually looking for Jeremy."

She raises an eyebrow.

"He's in his room, I think," Fiona says from the other side of the table. "At least he said something about studying."

"He's being a serious second year," Cyprus adds. "Do you think we'll be like that next year?"

"I don't think you'll ever be serious," Essie counters.

"Thanks, guys." I wave and leave them to their game, hurrying down the corridor until I get to Jeremy's door. I take a deep breath and lift my fist to knock, only for the door to swing open.

I stare at him for a moment, not knowing what to say.

Jeremy holds up his phone. "Cyprus messaged saying you were coming."

I nod, my mouth suddenly very dry and my words have escaped me.

"Do you want to come in?" he asks. "Or we can go for a walk if you want?"

I shake my head. "Here is fine."

Something like relief crosses his face. Which makes sense. If I had bad news for him, then I wouldn't want to be in his room.

I follow him inside and he shuts the door,

lingering for a moment as if deciding whether he should lock it or not.

"Do it," I say, finally managing to find my words. "You know what they're like when they're drinking. If you don't lock it, we'll end up with Essie in the middle of the room serenading us."

"Hmm, you have a point." He clicks it shut.

I look between his bed and his desk chair, trying to decide where it's best to sit. Eventually I decide that the bed looks the comfiest and perch myself on it, folding my hands in front of me on top of my blue and white skirt. Perhaps I should have changed out of my uniform before I came here, but I didn't want to waste any more time.

Jeremy sits next to me, but keeps a suitable amount of distance between us.

"Congratulations," he says. "You performed well."

"Thanks, but you know as well as I do that second is disappointing."

He chuckles. "True, but you get to try again in the next round at least."

"We do." I fiddle with the hem of my skirt. "I liked that you came to watch us," I admit.

"Well, I came to watch you."

"I know." I bite my bottom lip, trying to find the words to say what I want to. "Did you mean what you said earlier?"

"Which part?"

"About not wanting to just be my friend." I look up at him, realising that I probably look more vulnerable than I'm completely comfortable with.

But this is Jeremy. I have no reason to worry about anything. He won't take advantage or reject me in a way that will be unnecessarily cruel.

"I meant it," he says softly. "I know it's not what you want..."

"It is" I blurt, not wanting him to say something that he doesn't actually believe. "I thought I was making the right decision, but I've been more distracted thinking about not being distracted by you."

Jeremy chuckles. "I can see how that would cause a problem."

"So, I guess what I'm saying is would you like to go on a date with me? Or are we past that? I'm not really sure how this is supposed to go," I ramble.

His whole face lights up as if he's realised what I'm trying to say. "We can go wherever we want to," he responds. "Including out with the others, if you want?"

I shake my head. "I'd rather stay in with you if that's okay? Unless you need to do the serious second-year work they were teasing you about in the kitchen."

"My *serious* work was not wanting to be drinking when you came back in case you wanted to continue our talk," he admits.

"Oh." My heart skips a beat. "Then you're free?"

He nods. "Are you hungry?"

"Yes. And I'm dying for a pizza. Zara told us not to eat any for the past week."

"I could go for pizza. I can order some while you shower if you want?"

I raise an eyebrow. "Are you trying to tell me that I smell?"

Alarm flits through his eyes, meaning he probably hasn't worked out that I'm only joking.

I reach out and place a hand on his arm. "It's okay, I know you're just guessing because you know what you feel like after a game."

"I didn't mean anything by it."

"I know you didn't. I thought about showering first, but I didn't want to waste any more time than I already have." I get to my feet and stand a little awkwardly in the middle of his room, unsure what to do with myself. "I won't be long." I gesture towards the door but don't move.

He nods.

I take a deep breath and start to head over to it.

"Krissi," he says, getting to his feet.

I turn instantly, bringing us very close together.

Jeremy reaches out and brushes a strand of hair out of my face, the touch leaving a faint tingle along my skin.

I step forward, bringing us flush with one another and wrap my arms around his neck. There's not going to be any doubt about who started *this* kiss.

His hand settles on my lower back, pulling me closer, and then his lips are on mine.

My eyes flutter closed and my whole body relaxes as I give in to the kiss I've been thinking about almost constantly since the first time we did this. I'm not sure how I ever thought I could avoid being distracted by him.

We break apart but don't move away from one another. My gaze fixates on his and I can see the torrent of emotions in his eyes.

"I've wanted to do that again since the first time," he says, his voice hoarse and low.

"Me too," I admit. "I'm sorry it took so long for me to come around."

Jeremy lets out a low laugh. "I don't think this counts as so long."

I count back the weeks in my head and end up joining his amusement. "All right, maybe not that long. But thank you for giving me the space I needed to come to my own conclusions."

"You're welcome, but I don't think I'll be doing it again," he jokes.

"I don't plan on doing it again."

"Do I have to start lying to you about how graceful you are when you're a leopard now?" he teases.

"Oh no, I'm aware of what a disaster zone I am when I'm shifted. But I feel a bit more confident about it after the course you suggested."

"I'm glad."

"Can we do it again sometime?"

He nods. "There are probably some courses that we can look into if it's something you really want to do."

"I think I do. But partly because I had a lot of fun with you."

He grins. "Then your wish is my command."

"You're a tiger not a genie."

"I could be both."

"You know that's not how being turned works," I counter.

He cocks his head to the side. "Are genies turned beings?"

I shrug. "I don't actually know, but I've always assumed it was like vampires and mer where some genies are born that way, and others are turned by a curse. But I've never met one and you know how secretive they can be."

"I do. But you know what isn't secretive?"

"Mmm?"

"What you like on your pizzas. A meat feast with barbecue sauce, right?"

I'm not sure if he's guessing, or if he just paid attention last time we had pizza. "You've got it."

"All right, I'll order and go pick it up. Anything else you want?"

"Cookie dough ice cream?"

"Zara really has been cracking the whip."

I laugh lightly. "Mmhmm. Plus we lost out on first place and I kind of want to eat my feelings but in a way that makes you think I'm cute."

"I already think you're cute."

"Then my mission is complete." I go up on my toes and kiss his cheek. "I'll be back soon."

"I look forward to it."

I unlock his door and step out into the corridor, already feeling lighter than I did before. I finally made the move I've wanted to ever since we first kissed.

No, that's not right. Since we first met.

And I'm looking forward to finding out more of what I've been missing. Starting with our date tonight.

Krissi

I HURRY out of my room, already a bit worried about how long it took me to shower and choose what to wear. Which is ridiculous when my choice has landed on an oversized t-shirt and a pair of comfortable shorts. Maybe I should be putting more of an effort on, but I figure that Jeremy has already seen me hanging around the flat in some less than flattering combinations of loungewear, he doesn't care what I'm wearing.

"Hey, Krissi," Bernie says from down the corridor, stopping me in my tracks.

"Hey, I didn't realise you were around."

She nods. "I just got in from my lecture and am going to join the others now." She gestures to the kitchen. "I take it you're not coming."

"No. I'm hanging out with Jeremy."

Surprise flits across her face. "Really?"

"Mmhmm."

"In shorts that small?"

I look down. "They're no shorter than my cheerleading skirt."

Bernie snorts. "Yes, but you're wearing them to go spend time with a guy you like."

A furious blush rises to my cheeks and she starts laughing almost instantly.

"I see."

"You don't see anything."

"I'm a vampire, Krissi, I can sense changes in your blood flow very easily and from a great distance."

"You realise how creepy that sounds, right?"

A small smile lifts at Bernie's lips. "Yes, but I'm hoping you won't hold it against me. Oh, hey, I meant to mention that I signed up for cooking classes like you suggested. They start next week."

"Oh, that's great. I hope they help with the blood drinking."

"Me too."

A loud shout comes from the kitchen, drawing our attention to it.

"I should go change so I can join them," she says. "Have a fun date."

"I will."

"Oh wow, you're not even going to deny that's what it is."

"Nope, I'm not." I grin. "And you can tell Mickie that too so she doesn't give me one of her disapproving looks in the morning."

Bernie lets out an amused laugh. "It'll be the first thing I tell her."

I say goodbye and head back to Jeremy's room, knocking once before pushing the door open and stepping inside.

He's been busy while I showered, setting up a bunch of cushions on the bed so they can face the screen, and with a steaming cup of tea ready and waiting for me next to a couple of pizza boxes.

"I had help," he admits.

"You didn't let Mickie make the tea, did you?" I ask, eyeing it suspiciously.

He chuckles. "No, Essie did it."

"Oh, good, it's safe to drink, then." A loud shout comes from the kitchen next door and I wince. "Is it always this loud?"

He nods. "Maybe we should have done this in

your room."

"Maybe, but it'll be fine, they'll be leaving soon." I don't wait for him to say anything and sit on the bed, shuffling backwards so I'm leaning against some of the cushions.

Jeremy's smile makes my heart flutter. "What did you want to watch by the way?"

"Oh, I hadn't thought about that," I admit. "I kind of assumed we wouldn't be doing much actual watching."

He nods, seeming to understand. "Have you ever seen *Reap Me On A Sunday*?"

"Is there anyone alive who hasn't? It's one of the most popular supernatural sitcoms ever."

He clicks a couple of times and the familiar opening sequence starts to play. It's a good choice. I've seen it enough times that it won't matter if we dip in and out of the show.

"I refused to watch it for years," Jeremy admits as he hands me one of the pizza boxes and gets onto the bed beside me.

"Why?" I flip open the lid, enjoying the comforting scent of hot gooey cheese and barbecue sauce.

"I thought I wouldn't like it because it has a reaper lead."

"And now you're good friends with a reaper," I

point out.

"I never had anything against them," he says quickly. "I just thought I wouldn't be able to relate much to the main character. Please don't tell Dylan that? I've never told anyone that before."

"Your secret is safe with me," I promise. I take a bite of pizza and let out a small satisfied hum. "This is good."

"I'd say thanks, but you know I didn't make it."

"You still picked the right flavour."

"And there's cookie dough ice cream in the freezer too," he promises.

"How are you still single?" My brain catches up with my mouth. "Oh. Right."

Jeremy chuckles. "Well there's this cute cheerleader who keeps telling me that she just wants to be friends, but I can't stop thinking about kissing her."

I join his laughter and set my pizza aside. "I heard the cute cheerleader told you she'd changed her mind."

"Hmm, she did," Jeremy agrees. Tentatively, he reaches out and puts his arm around me.

I shuffle closer on the bed so I'm leaning against him. Neither of us says anything as we sit comfortably and watch a bit of the show. Not that I'm really taking any of it in. Every part of me is hyper-focused on the way Jeremy's hand is absent-mindedly stroking my arm, and how comfortable the whole situation feels. I can't believe I convinced myself I didn't want this.

"So, I have something to ask you," Jeremy says after a bit.

"Oh?"

An impish smile flits over his face. "Will you come to my game on Wednesday?"

I let out a soft snort. "You already know I'll be there," I point out. "We're scheduled to be cheering for you guys, remember?"

"But do I get to tell the rest of the team that my girlfriend is watching?" he asks, a little more serious than before.

"Yes." The word slips out before I even give myself time to think about it.

One of his eyebrows quirks upwards. "I half expected you to say no."

"Me too," I admit. "But I don't think there's any point in keeping it quiet. Most people we know seem to have an opinion on whether we should be together already." Which reminds me that I need to message Grace and see if she's around tomorrow for coffee. I know she'll want all the details about what's happened since I left her earlier.

"That's fair. I think I just expected you to want to be more careful in case this doesn't work out."

I nod, understanding where he's coming from, but certain it's the right move still. "I don't see this ending any time soon." I can't believe I'm saying this to him, but it doesn't feel like we're starting at the beginning of dating, we've known each other too long for that.

And he's seen me shifted. Not many people can claim that. Except for several of my flatmates. Somehow, I've shifted in front of more people while at Obscure Academy than in the five years prior.

"I don't think it will either," he agrees. "Want that ice cream now?"

"Only if you'll bring two spoons."

"I wasn't going to let you eat it all yourself," he assures me.

"Good."

He leans in and kisses me softly on the lips before getting up and heading to the door.

I watch him go, a satisfied feeling settling within me as everything slots into place. Having a boyfriend isn't going to mean that I can't focus on cheerleading and my studies, it just means I'll have someone to support me from the sidelines at competitions, and help me with concepts I'm struggling to grasp for my classes.

This way, I get the best of all of it, and I couldn't ask for more.

Krissi

THE WHISTLE BLOWS, signalling the end of the game and another win for the Obscure Academy rugby team. We explode into action, cheering and shouting for their victory as loud as we can until the ref signals for us to stop so he can deal with the opposing teams.

Grace sighs from beside me, her hands on her hips despite the two large blue pom-poms in her hands.

"You all right?" I ask.

"Mmhmm, just admiring the rugby players," she

responds. "Those shorts really don't leave much to the imagination."

"Grace!" I half-scold.

"What? It's true. One look and you can imagine exactly what's going on underneath."

"I don't need to imagine," I mutter.

Her eyes widen and her attention shoots to me. "I'm sorry, what?"

"You heard me."

"Krissi! You've been officially dating for a week."

I shrug. "So? You're the one who kept pointing out we've been dancing around one another for months. That all counts too. Besides, you don't have to be in a relationship to sleep with someone."

"I know I don't, but this is you we're talking about," she responds. "I guess I just expected you to wait."

"I'm glad I didn't."

"Mmhmm, from the way those shorts fit, I'm not surprised." She wiggles her eyebrows, though I can tell she's gone from admiration to teasing.

"I hope you realise I'm going to be insufferable when you start dating someone."

She snorts. "I'd like to see you try. You don't have an insufferable bone in your body."

"Try me."

"Those are fighting words when you're up against

a pixie. I can make life very annoying." The mischief in her eyes convinces me of the truth behind her words. But I'm willing to risk it.

"Hello, Grace," Jeremy says, making us both jump. I hadn't noticed the rugby team heading over to us.

"Hi, Jeremy. I'm going to go talk to Jazz now." She waves and disappears, leaving the two of us to have a moment alone.

Jeremy slips an arm around my waist and I lean in, easily exchanging affection with him even in front of everyone else.

"You played a good game," I say.

"Do you mean that or are you just guessing?"

I let out a small laugh. "A bit of both. I've watched enough rugby games to be able to tell when something is good, but I don't know the rules well enough to actually understand what it all means."

"That's fair," he agrees. "It's how I felt when I was watching you cheer. You were doing all these things that looked good, but I couldn't tell what was good or bad in terms of the competition."

"Maybe we can try and explain it to one another?" I suggest. "That way we can actually understand each others' sports."

"I'd like that. I'm sure you won't like it if I suddenly start talking about pom-pom shaking and waving your hands in the air."

"I don't mind what you call the moves." I place a hand on his chest and look up at him, hoping that he's reassured by the gesture. "I already appreciate that you want to support me."

"The same goes for you if you want to call it a ball toss thingy."

"I already know that's called a pass. But point taken."

"Krissi, Jeremy!" Grace calls. "We're all going for drinks. Are you two coming?"

I look up at him. "I'm game if you are."

"Then let's go."

"Okay, but if I drink too much, I'm going to need you to find me a safe place where I can shift without breaking any laws," I warn him.

"Preferably one with crash pads on the floor and walls," he mutters.

"Oh, definitely." Amusement dances behind my words. "Worried you've bitten off more than you can chew?"

"Not in the slightest."

My eyes flutter closed as he leans in and presses his lips against mine. I wrap my arms around him, pulling him closer and deepening the kiss. I'm vaguely aware of a whistle coming from the direction of our teams, but I don't pay it any attention.

We break apart, both grinning wildly and head

over to join everyone else with our hands entwined. There's a skip in my step that wasn't there before, and I plan on enjoying every minute of it.

* * *

Thank you for reading *Shifting Forms For Clumsy Shifters*, I hope you enjoyed it! If you want to learn about what Bernie gets up to when she attends cooking classes to try and deal with her dislike of drinking blood, then you can in the next book in the series, *Drinking Blood For Squeamish Vampires*: http://books2read.com/drinkingbloodforsqueamishvampires And if you want to find out what happens when Krissi & Jeremy attend one of Kayra's balls, you can download a free bonus scene here: https://books.authorlauragreenwood.co.uk/yvgu2efwtd (Grace's story is coming later in the series! Read on to the Author Note for more about it!)

Thank you for reading *Shifting Forms For Clumsy Felines*, I hope you enjoyed it!

The *Obscure Academy* series will continue with other characters from the academy, and will focus on a different couple and supernatural type in each book. All of Krissi and Jeremy's flatmates (apart from Craig) have books planned, along with Grace and some of the other characters. All of the books will be light-hearted and fun and are loosely inspired by my own time at university - though sadly I can't say that any of the people I lived with were secretly vampires (though Craig *is* named after an invisible flatmate I had during my first year - we knew his name, but we never actually saw him). That includes the game the flatmates played - Ring Of Fire. It's a fairly popular drinking game that often has different rules depending on who you're playing with. In this case, I mostly used the rules my friends and I used, but I also included some that my partner used to play.

If you're wanting more from the cheer squad and their continuing on in the competition, then it'll be coming! Grace's book (*Minor Inconveniences For Annoyed Pixies*) is planned as book six of the *Obscure Academy* series, and I also plan for one of the books to follow Zara (but I haven't settled on a title yet!)

If you've already read my complete *Sabre Woods Academy* series, then you may have met Jeremy before. If not, he's a side character who becomes friends with the main character, Kayra, after her mother tries to insist they get engaged. If you like big cats and academy, that's the way to go!

In chapter thirteen, Bernie talks about the synthetic blood inside the *City of Blood*, you can read more about the events in the dystopian vampire-run city in the series of the same name, and in *The Black Fan* series.

If you want to keep up to date with new releases and other news, you can join my Facebook Reader Group or mailing list.

Stay safe & happy reading!

- Laura

Signed Paperback & Merchandise:

You can find signed paperbacks, hardcovers, and merchandise based on my series (including stickers, magnets, face masks, and more!) via my website: https://www.authorlauragreenwood.co.uk/p/shop.html

Series List:

* denotes a completed series

THE OBSCURE WORLD

A paranormal & urban fantasy world where supernaturals live out in the open alongside humans. Each series can be read on its own, but there are cameos from past characters and mentions of previous events.

Ashryn Barker* - Grimalkin Academy: Kittens* - Grimalkin Academy: Catacombs* - City Of Blood* - Grimalkin Vampires* - Supernatural Retrieval Agency* - The Black Fan - Sabre Woods Academy* - Scythe Grove Academy* - The Shifter Season - Cauldron Coffee Shop - Broomstick Bakery - Obscure Academy - Stonerest Academy - Obscure World: Holidays - Harker Academy

THE FORGOTTEN GODS WORLD

A fantasy romance world based on Egyptian mythology. Each series can be read on its own, but there are cameos from past characters and mentions of previous events.

The Queen of Gods* - Forgotten Gods - Forgotten Gods: Origins*

THE EGYPTIAN EMPIRE

A modern fantasy world set in an alternative timeline where the Egyptian Empire never fell.

The Apprentice Of Anubis

THE GRIMM WORLD

A fantasy fairy tale romance world. Each series can be

read on its own, but there are cameos from past characters and mentions of previous events.

Grimm Academy* - Fate Of The Crown* - Once Upon An Academy* - The Princess Competition

* * *

THE PARANORMAL COUNCIL WORLD

A paranormal romance & urban fantasy world where paranormals are hidden away from the human world, and are in search of their fated mates. Each series can be read on its own, but there are cameos from past characters and mentions of previous events.

The Paranormal Council Series* - The Fae Queens* - Paranormal Criminal Investigations* - MatchMater Paranormal Dating App* - The Necromancer Council* - Return Of The Fae*

* * *

OTHER SERIES

Beyond The Curse - Untold Tales* - The Dragon Duels* -

Rosewood Academy - ME* - Speed Dating With The Denizens Of The Underworld (shared world) - Seven Wardens* (co-written with Skye MacKinnon) - Tales Of Clan Robbins (co-written with L.A. Boruff) -

Firehouse Witches* (co-written with Lacey Carter Andersen & L.A. Boruff) - Purple Oasis (co-written series with Arizona Tape) - Valentine Pride* (co-written with L.A. Boruff) - Magic and Metaphysics Academy* (co-written with L.A. Boruff)

* * *

TWIN SOULS UNIVERSE

A paranormal romance & urban fantasy world co-written with Arizona Tape. Each series can be read on its own, but there are cameos from past characters and mentions of previous events.

Twin Souls* - Dragon Soul* - The Renegade Dragons* - The Vampire Detective* - Amethyst's Wand Shop Mysteries - The Necromancer Morgue Mysteries

ABOUT THE AUTHOR

Laura is a USA Today Bestselling Author of paranormal, fantasy, urban fantasy, and contemporary romance. When she's not writing, she drinks a lot of tea, tries to resist French macarons, and works towards a diploma in Egyptology. She lives in the UK, where most of her books are set. Laura specialises in quick reads, whether you're looking for a swoonworthy romance for the bath, or an action-packed adventure for your latest journey, you'll find the perfect match amongst her books!

FOLLOW THE AUTHOR

- Website: www.authorlauragreenwood.co.uk
- Mailing List: www.authorlauragreenwood.co.uk/p/mailing-list-sign-up.html
- Facebook Group: http://facebook.com/groups/theparanormalcouncil

- Facebook Page: http://facebook.com/authorlauragreenwood
- Bookbub: www.bookbub.com/authors/laura-greenwood

www.ingramcontent.com/pod-product-compliance
Lightning Source LLC
Chambersburg PA
CBHW020926160726
47993CB00005B/2147